"Luli. My grandmother intended you would be looked after. That's proof of it." Gabriel pointed back to the billionaires found to be not quite good enough for Mae's surrogate daughter.

"She wanted to hand me to a stranger like I'm a...a thing." Her eyes were bright and angry.

"I don't think that's true." He had taunted her earlier that she was one more asset he was inheriting, though. And he might not need this inheritance from Mae, but if he intended to accept it, he had to take all of it—including the treasure she had confined to this house like an heirloom jewel tucked in a safe.

His grandmother had valued Luli highly enough to think her good enough for her only grandson. For that reason alone, he couldn't throw Luli away.

"You'll honor the dowry if I marry one of them?" she asked with dread, glancing at the papers with desperation and anguish.

Repulsion gripped him at the thought of gnarled hands setting themselves against those luscious curves. If anyone touched her, he wanted it to be *him*.

"No. I want you to marry *me*."

Canadian **Dani Collins** knew in high school that she wanted to write romance for a living. Twenty-five years later, after marrying her high school sweetheart, having two kids with him, working at several generic office jobs and submitting countless manuscripts, she got The Call. Her first Harlequin novel won the Reviewers' Choice Award for Best First in Series from *RT Book Reviews*. She now works in her own office, writing romance.

Visit the Author Profile page
at Harlequin.com for more titles.

Dani Collins

—

UNTOUCHED UNTIL HER ULTRA-RICH HUSBAND

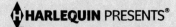

Recycling programs
for this product may
not exist in your area.

ISBN-13: 978-1-335-53838-3

Untouched Until Her Ultra-Rich Husband

First North American publication 2019

Copyright © 2019 by Dani Collins

Printed in U.S.A.

UNTOUCHED UNTIL HER ULTRA-RICH HUSBAND

This book is dedicated to my son Sam and his schoolmate Luli. Sam mentioned Luli on a call home and I said, "I like her name. I might steal it for a heroine." He said, "It's actually Lucrecia." I said, "Even better." I later had the good fortune to meet Luli and she's lovely. Along with her name, I lifted Luli's vocation of computer programming and the fact her heritage is Venezuelan. The real Luli, however, has much nicer parents.

CHAPTER ONE

BORN IN THE Year of the Dragon, Gabriel Dean was dominant, ambitious, passionate and willing to take risks. He jumped for no one.

His signature detachment, however, was not impervious to his grandmother's ringtone.

The distinctive tinkle of a brass tea bell might have struck some as a sign of affection. And yes, he had seen her shake such a bell on two of the three occasions he had spoken to her in person, but sentiment was not a gene either of them possessed.

No, the bell was a practical choice, being odd enough to draw his attention no matter what was going on around him. Mae Chen's missives were financial in nature, time sensitive and always lucrative. He didn't need more money, but he hadn't joined the eleven zeroes club at thirty by ignoring opportunities to make more.

Therefore, at the first peal, he held up a finger to pause the roundtable discussion of an energy takeover that would make him the de facto owner of a small country. He turned his titanium smartphone onto its custom-made back and touched the sapphire crystal screen.

Transmitted from Luli: Your grandmother has experienced a medical event. Her instructions in such case are to promptly advise you that you are her designated heir. Contact details for her physician are below.

That was new information.

In one fluid move, he tagged the doctor's number, picked up the phone and rose to leave without explanation. He moved with purpose from the room, more disturbed by the label heir than by his grandmother's condition.

For one thing, Mae was far too bellicose to suffer anything for long, particularly ill health. She would be on her feet before this call was picked up.

As for Gabriel being her heir, she wouldn't stipulate such a thing without attaching a symphony's worth of strings. She had been trying to maneuver him into a beholden state for two decades. It was the reason he had kept his interest in her fortune objective and made no assumptions about his entitlement to it. He religiously returned her invitations to invest with equally advantageous opportunities of his own. Tit for tat, scoop for scoop. No obligations incurred on either side beyond reciprocal courtesy.

"A stroke," the doctor advised him seconds later. "It's unlikely she will survive."

Her transfer to the private clinic had been swift and discreet, the doctor continued.

"I expect this will cause ripples through the financial districts when it's announced? I didn't know *you* were her grandson."

While Gabriel's agile brain sifted through the implications of his grandmother being incapacitated, possibly disappearing from his life altogether, the inquisitiveness of the physician's tone penetrated. He could hear the man's thoughts buzzing like an annoying mosquito. Buy? Sell? Were there properties that could be snatched up before they were officially on the market? How could the fine doctor take advantage of this news before anyone else?

Thanks to their mutual exchange of information over the years, Mae had expanded from relatively stable investments in real estate to tech and renewable energy, precious metals and that fickle mistress—oil. None of that could be left without a sitter.

Gabriel assured the doctor he would be there as soon as possible. He messaged his executive assistant to reschedule the meeting he'd abandoned. He also told her to clear his calendar and notify his pilot to ready the jet. As he headed to the elevator, he glanced at the nearest face at a desk and said, "My car, please."

The woman quickly put her call on hold and his chauffeured Rolls-Royce Phantom arrived at the curb as he pushed through the revolving door at the bottom of his building.

The humidity of a New York summer hit him in the face, but it would be monsoon rains in Singapore. His butler kept his jet packed for all climes and occasions, though. His grandmother kept a room at her house for him, not that he had ever used it. Invitations had come periodically, maybe to discuss the fact she was designating him her heir. He also owned a building of flats in that city. The top one was designated for his use, so he never took his grandmother up on—

"Gabriel!" A woman moved into his path and dipped her sunglasses to reveal her fake lashes and waxed brows. "I thought you might like to take me to lunch. It's Tina," she reminded after a beat where he only stared, trying to place her. She splayed her hand on the upper swells of her breasts where they were revealed by her wide-necked blouse. "We met at my father's retirement party last weekend. You said you liked my song."

He must have been speaking out of politeness because he had no recollection of her voice, her father or the party.

"I'm traveling," he dismissed, and stepped around her.

If there was one thing he needed less than more money, it was another social climber throwing herself at him.

He slid onto a cool leather seat and his driver closed him into the air-conditioned interior.

Gabriel glanced at the square face of his gold Girard-Perregaux and calculated the approximate time until he would land.

Such affectations as vintage watches and Valentino briefcases meant nothing to him, but appearances mattered to everyone else. He always played to win, even at "who wears it best?" so he ordered hand-sewn suits in rare wools like vicuña and qiviut. He had his leather shoes lined with the softest materials when they were custom cobbled in Italy. He hung all of it off a body that he ruthlessly kept in peak athletic condition.

He wore sunscreen and moisturized.

And he genuinely didn't care that folding his grandmother's net worth into his own would tip him into the exalted echelon of world's first trillionaire. All it meant, quite inconveniently, was more work—yet another thing he didn't need.

His grandmother was his only relative of note, however, despite being both strange and estranged. He might lack strong feelings toward her or her money, but he did feel a responsibility to preserve her empire. He respected what she had built in her seventy years. He might be progressive by nature, but he didn't tear down institutions for the sake of it.

He flicked back to the original message and brought the phone to his chin as he dictated a text.

Who is Mae's business manager?

Transmitted from Luli: I assist Mrs. Chen in managing her transactions. May I help with a specific inquiry or instruction?

Artificial intelligence was so delightfully passive-aggressive, always deferential when it was being obstructive.

Send me the contact details of the man or

woman who carries out Mae's personal banking transactions.

Transmitted from Luli: I perform those tasks. How may I help?

Gabriel bit back a curse. Once this news was released and his connection to Mae Chen made public, a global circus would erupt around her financial holdings. The clock was already ticking, given her doctor had learned of their connection.

He switched gears and began sending instructions to his own team of advisors and brokers to reach out to hers. Once he was on the ground, he would learn exactly who ran things for Mae Chen and firmly take the reins from him.

"Luli." The butler introduced her last, since she had deliberately positioned herself at the end of the line of staff, after the housemaids and cook. She was practically standing around the corner of the house where vines grew against the wall that ensured the privacy of Mae Chen's colonial-era mansion.

His mansion now.

"You're human."

If she was, Gabriel Dean was the first to notice in her twenty-two years of existence.

Of course, Luli experienced very human reactions as she shook hands with Mae's grandson, bowing slightly and murmuring, "Sir," as she did. Her heart was pounding, her skin coated in cold perspiration, her stomach churning like a pit of snakes.

Aside from the married butler and the gardeners, she rarely saw men. Not this sort of man, especially. His black, glossy hair was precision-trimmed and disheveled with equal precision. He was clean-shaven, his cheekbones a masterpiece, his mouth—she didn't know what to compare it to, having never studied a man's lips before. They weren't the feminine peaks and sensual fullness with corner curls like hers. They were thinner, straighter and as much a statement of unspoken authority as the rest of him.

"Is that your full name? Luli?"

"Lucrecia," she provided, tacking on the other half of a name she had nearly forgotten. "Cruz."

His gaze flickered down her pleated-neck dress. Its straight cut was belted with the same pale yellow cotton and the hem ended just above her ankles, revealing her bare feet in sandals. The maids wore an apron over theirs and looked efficient and smart. Luli wished she had that extra layer of protection, but even a plate of armor wouldn't hide the fact she was significantly more endowed in the chest than the delicately built Malaysian women beside her. On her, the fabric pulled across her hips and required a higher slit to accommodate her longer stride.

Gabriel was taller than she had expected. No wonder Mae was always telling her to sit. It was intimidating to have someone look down on you.

Gabriel's gaze came back to her face, taking in features she knew to be striking. It wasn't just that her skin was paler than the rest of the staff's, or her eyes distinctly Caucasian. Her light brown hair was naturally streaked with ash blond and her nose slender and elegant.

Gabriel's eyelids were distinctly Asian, his irises an unexpected gray-green.

She had seen enough photos to expect him to be beautiful, but she had not expected this radiation of power. She should have. His grandmother possessed a version of it, but this man's force of will nearly knocked her off her feet and all he had done was step out of his car.

Now he relaxed his grip so she wasn't sure if the handshake was over. She took too long to draw her hand from his. It made her feel ignorant and foolish. The maids would be laughing at her later, but she couldn't help this weakness of fascination that overcame her.

"May we offer refreshments, sir?" the butler asked. "Your room has been prepared, if you wish to rest."

"I'm here to work." He glanced toward the front of the house. "Coffee will do."

"Of course." The butler clapped his hands to send everyone filing back to their duties.

Luli breathed out a subtle sigh of relief and started to follow.

"Luli." Gabriel's voice jolted her. "You'll show me to my grandmother's office."

He spoke English with an American accent, not the British one she was used to hearing and copying. He waved for her to join him as he climbed the front steps.

She was disturbed by it. She struggled to find acceptance here as it was. Mae gave her special treatment in some ways, but Luli never liked to do anything that made it seem as though she was *trying* to rise above everyone else.

Besides, her guilty conscience wasn't ready to confess to him what she'd done.

She concentrated on her breathing and maintaining a tall posture. She ensured her expression was serene, her movements graceful and unhurried despite her unsteady pulse and the shakiness brought on by sleep deprivation.

She had had twenty hours to react to this sudden change in her circumstance. It was her habit, through years of boredom and confinement, to mentally plan for every conceivable situation. Thus, she had known from the first call of alarm into the garden what she would have to do.

Executing those actions, however, had taken nerves of steel and hours of careful coding into the night. There was no room for error—and likely no forgiveness from this man no matter how things played out.

Gabriel paused inside the opulent foyer, taking in the mosaic tiles beneath their feet, the inlaid wood in the stair banister, the priceless art and the arrangements of fresh flowers. All his now.

Luli halted as well, waiting until he glanced at her expectantly.

"Mrs. Chen's office is the third door," she murmured with a nod toward the hallway.

In a confusing war of chivalry against her effort to be subservient, he waited for her to go first then fell into step beside her.

"I'm very sorry about your grandmother," she said. "We'll miss her deeply."

"It sounds like it was very swift."

It had been. They'd all known the quick, anxious efforts of Mae's nurse were futile. Even as Mae's helicopter had airlifted her from the garden where it had happened, a blanket of subdued reflection had hung over the entire house.

Luli brought him into Mae's office. The room was designed along spare lines, more staid than the other rooms, but still had feminine touches in the pastel color scheme and the English teapot that Luli filled for both of them every afternoon.

It felt terribly empty in here. Who would she drink tea with now? What was going to happen?

Her future was no longer in the tight, but secure hands of Mae Chen. Luli could kid herself that she was taking her destiny into her own hands, but that wasn't true. The way this man reacted once he learned what she had done would dictate how the rest of her life proceeded.

His hands were long-fingered and lightly tanned. They looked powerful. Deadly.

Luli stood beside the rolling chair at the delicate writing desk that was her workstation, waiting for him to sit. He took in the room, glancing beyond the windows to the garden, and gave each painting and vase a brief, incisive glance.

She found herself holding her breath, waiting for his assessing gaze to come back to her, hoping for a sign of approachability in him. Approval on some level. Something that would reassure her.

"I thought you were a form of AI, but there's nothing artificial about you. Is there?" His head turned and his expression eased, revealing a slant of something that invited and appreciated, even as it caused her inner radar to tingle with caution.

She had the most bizarre sensation of being chased, breaths growing uneven despite not moving. Her middle filled with fluttering butterflies, but they weren't fear. They were the excitement of the unknown. Of playful pursuit.

This was sexual awareness, she realized with a pressure in her throat that was an urge to both laugh and scream. She understood sexual attraction in a very abstract way. She had been exposed to the feminine tricks of making herself appealing to the opposite sex far too young, but she wasn't trying any of them right now. She was barefaced and the only reason she stood tall and sucked in her stomach was in an effort to seem confident and competent.

And she had been judged on her external attributes from an early age, but hadn't *felt* it, not like this. If anything, she'd been repulsed by older men studying her and assigning her a score. Occasionally, since being here, one of Mrs. Chen's visitors had noticed her and made a remark before she was shooed out of sight. She had been an odd duck, if not an outright ugly duckling.

She hadn't realized a man's gaze could make her stomach wobble and her blood feel as though it fizzed in her veins. That a force field could encompass her like a cup over a spider, so she could be scooped into the palm of his hand to be crushed or freed on his whim.

The butler came in with the tray, breaking their locked gaze.

"How shall I prepare your *kopi*, Mr. Dean?" the butler asked, pouring from the carafe into a jade-green cup with a gold handle that he balanced on its matching saucer.

"Black." His sharp gaze touched on the single cup and swung back to Luli. "You're not having any?"

The butler didn't react, but Luli read the servant's affront in the angle of his shoulders and the stiffness beneath his impassive expression. They'd been at war for years because she had Mae's confidence in ways he didn't. He'd been incensed that he had learned from *Luli* who Mrs. Chen's grandson was—*after* Luli had informed Gabriel.

What could Luli have said, though? *She doesn't trust you. She doesn't trust men.* Mae had encouraged Luli to trust no one but her and Luli had given her the loyalty that Mae craved.

None of which changed the fact that if the butler had to fetch Luli a cup right now, he would *die*.

If she was a small person, she would force him to do it, but she was saving her energy for a greater revolt. A more daunting target.

"You're very kind," she murmured. "But that's not necessary."

"The bell is here if you require anything further, Mr. Dean," the butler said, glancing darkly toward Luli before he closed the door firmly on his way out.

Gabriel waved at the arrangement of sofa and chairs, all upholstered in silk brocade, and waited for her to lower onto a cushion before he sat across from her.

Honestly, this regard he was extending to her was laughable. Her conscience writhed as she folded her hands in her lap. He was going to explode when he realized how undeserving she was of this respect.

Despite the fact she would have to take control of the discussion eventually, she waited for him to lead. There were so many ways this could go, some of them life altering—maybe even life-threatening. Her research had revealed he was a black belt in kung fu. Her morning tai chi in the courtyard with Mae and the rest of the household was no match for the lightning-fast and lethal moves he no doubt possessed.

"After signing papers at the hospital, I met with my grandmother's attorney," he informed her. "My power of attorney was finalized so I could assume the helm during probate. A press release has been issued to announce our connection. Legally and publicly it is accepted that I have taken possession of Chen Enterprises. Yet, when I arrived at the head office, very few of my instructions could be fully executed. I was told that every instruction and transaction goes through Luli."

He sipped his coffee while his gaze stayed pinned on her.

"They couldn't even run me a comprehensive list of her assets and accounts, so I could begin contacting the banks for access."

A coal of heat burned in her center, but she said nothing, knowing that stammering out explanations when he hadn't yet asked a question would betray her nerves.

"You realize I'm not the only person under the impression you're a sophisticated task-management app?"

"I believe that is the impression your grandmother preferred to cultivate."

"Why?" His voice was whip sharp. She had to concentrate not to flinch as it landed on her.

"Among other things, it forces people to express themselves in writing," she explained in an unruffled tone. "It creates a traceable trail. She told me once that when your grandfather died, his business manager attempted to take advantage of her. She wasn't able to prove his wrongdoing and she wasn't able to take control of the wealth she had inherited. Not without a terrible fight."

"Those who don't learn from history are doomed to repeat it. Apparently."

Bam-bam-bam. Her heart threatened to crack open her breastbone.

"Since then, it has been her practice to maintain tight oversight with regard to her finances. She personally approves all but the most routine transactions."

"Does she? Because it sounds like *you* do."

"She didn't care for computers. I work under her direction." And steered her direction, when opportunities presented, but that wasn't important right now.

"Your actions strike me as empire building." He crossed his legs, hitching his pants as he did. "You have made yourself indispensable in a grasp for power. I've seen it before, many times."

"I have no empire," she assured him.

His cynical look said he saw right through her, which shouldn't cause her stomach to bottom out, but it did. He was nothing to her, but it was taking every ounce of courage she possessed to hold his gaze.

It struck her that she had never had the courage to defy Mae. What chance did that give her against someone like *him*?

"You live here?" The cynical twitch of his mesmerizing mouth called her a parasite.

"A room is assigned to me, yes."

"Where did you come from?"

"Venezuela."

"That wasn't what I was asking, but I hear that in your accent now." His gaze shifted as he took in her features once again. "It's sultry. Exotic."

He sounded vaguely mocking, which stung. Her rudimentary English, taught to her by a chaperone, had been perfected here, where Mae had learned it from a British boarding school. The staff spoke broken versions peppered with Indian, Malay and Pilipino accents.

As he stared at her, the tingle of sensual, elemental awareness shimmered around her again, disconcerting her. Logically, she presumed she could use her voice and looks to charm and distract him, but she had no practice wielding those weapons. Instead, she found herself fascinated by the subtle inflections in his voice and the slightest twitch of his lips.

"How long have you been here?" he asked.

"Eight years."

"Not Singapore. In this house, employed by my grandmother."

"I came to this house when I came to Singapore eight years ago."

He frowned. "How old are you?"

"Twenty-two."

"Were you hired as a housemaid?" He was taken aback. "How did you come to be doing high-level work like this?" He jerked his chin toward the sleeping laptop on the writing desk.

She licked her lips. How to explain?

"As I said, your grandmother found computers tiresome, but she wished to be as hands-on as possible with every facet of her business."

"You're her hands?"

He was skeptical, but it was true. Luli couldn't count the number of times Mae had nudged her in the back of the shoulder and told her, *Go back. Show me that again.*

"I perform various confidential tasks at her direction."

"Bank transfers, stock purchases...?"

"Yes. If a broker or middleman is used, I follow up after transmitting requests to ensure the task has been completed. I compile background information on potential employees and business partners, assist her in reviewing performance reports and run random secondary checks on various budgets and accounts, helping spot discrepancies that could point to misuse."

"People love audits, especially random ones. I bet you're very popular." He was being sarcastic.

"A necessary evil" was probably the kindest thing she'd been called, usually in an email chain not meant for her eyes.

Was she evil? She would have called her mother that, until she had been backed into a corner herself and now had to think about how *she* would survive.

"As you say, most people think I'm a computer program. I've never concerned myself much with whether people *like* me so long as your grandmother was satisfied with my work."

A small lie. She would love a friend, a real one, not an old woman who had forgotten what it was like to be young and curious about the world. One who was scared to let her see any of it, in case it made her leave.

"On the topic of programs," she said, feeling clammy sweat break on her palms. "It might interest you to know that your grandmother requested I switch exclusively to using your operating system. She had reservations about cloud-based so she purchased the download versions. We use all your business modules, accounting and security, the productivity suite... She wanted to know her most important records and cryptocurrency were backed up and protected against intrusion. She liked that you claim it's next to impossible to hack. I'm sure *you* could get in, though. If you had to."

There. She was inching onto the limb she had chosen.

It might hold her or it might snap and send her plummeting to her death.

CHAPTER TWO

LUCRECIA. IT SOUNDED like the Latin name for one of those exotic flowers found in remote jungles. The kind with waxy petals in shades of ivory streaked with lush crimson and mysterious indigo. The kind with a perfume that drew a bee inexorably into her honey trap.

Where she paralyzed and ate him alive.

What a way to go. Gabriel almost didn't see a downside, except that he'd learned very early not to fall for any sort of manipulation. They'd all been tried—threats, flattery, guilt, false friendship and—frequently—lust. Sex was something he enjoyed like whiskey over rocks or a cool swim on a hot day. It wasn't something he needed or succumbed to.

Yet this woman had put a coil of tension in him merely by existing and was notching it with each lift of her thick, curled lashes over her piercing blue-green eyes.

To think, he had only come to the house as a last resort, thinking he would fire up his grandmother's laptop and ascertain exactly what this "Luli" software was all about.

Her wares were soft, all right. In all the right places, despite being draped in the least flattering dress imaginable. The color was wrong for her skin tone, but there was no hiding her catwalk height or her flawless complexion. She didn't need makeup or adornments. In his mind, she only had to remove that dress and the pins from her hair and she would be perfect.

But she was his employee, he reminded himself, in the same way the workforce of any company became his responsibility and resource after a takeover.

Therefore, while he enjoyed fantasizing each time she threw one of those doe-eyed, speculative glances his way, looking ever so innocent as she let the tip of her tongue dampen her lips suggestively, he refused to let her see it was having the desired effect on him, i.e., *Desire*.

He definitely didn't let his carnal reaction blind him to the nuanced threat she was making.

"Why would I need to hack into accounts that belong to me?" he asked, muscles activating as though preparing to face an opponent on the mat.

"You wouldn't…"

If.

She didn't say it, but he heard the lilt of suggestion in the way she trailed off.

He set aside his half-finished coffee with a click of bone china meeting lacquered wood.

She swallowed, eyes shielded by her lashes, but she was watching him through them. Cautious. Scared, even.

He let his lip curl to let her know he was amused by her adorable attempt to extort from him.

"You understand I could have you arrested." Which was a strangely appalling thing to imagine. He had brought charges to bear in the past, when laws had been broken. He never thought twice about protecting himself and always sought justice through due process.

But there were exceptions to every rule, he supposed. Even the rules he made for himself.

"You could bring in the police," she agreed in that same trailing tone. This time the adjunct was *but*. "I haven't done anything illegal, though. Not yet."

Not *yet*? "Ah. You've planted a cyberbomb." He ought to be furious, but he was so flabbergasted by her audacity, he wanted to laugh. Did she know who he *was*?

"May we call them incentives?" Her gaze came up, crystal as the Caribbean Sea. Placid and appealing and full of sharks and deadly jellyfish with stinging tendrils.

His divided mind wanted to watch the shift of color in those eyes as he immersed himself in her even as the other half absorbed the word *incentives. Plural.*

"Call them anything you like. I'm calling the police." Even he didn't know whether he was bluffing. He took longer than he needed to bring his phone from his pocket, though, watching for her next move.

"If I don't log in soon, a tell-all will release to the press."

"Has my grandmother been running an opium den? What terrible tales could you possibly have to tell about her?" As far as he knew, Mae Chen's worst crime was being stubbornly resentful of her daughter's choice in husband—and rightfully so.

Luli's face went blank. "I'd rather not reveal it."

"Because you have nothing."

"Because your grandmother's good name would be smeared and she's been good to me."

"Yet you'll destroy her reputation to get what you want from me."

"I'll tell the truth." Her tone was grave, her comportment calm enough to make him think she might have something more than threats of revealing a dodgy tax write-off or a penchant for young men in small bathing suits.

"Something to do with my mother?"

"Not at all." That seemed to surprise her.

"What then? I'm not playing twenty questions."

She pinched her mouth together and glanced toward the door to ensure it was firmly closed.

"Human trafficking and forcible confinement."

"Ha!"

She didn't laugh.

"That's a very ugly accusation." There was a thriving black market in everything from drugs to kidneys, but it wasn't a shop on Fifth Avenue where women in their golden years could drop in and buy house staff. "Who? You?"

She swallowed. "Ask anyone here how many times I've been outside the front door of this house. They'll tell you today was the first time in eight years."

"Because you've coached them to say that? Are you ring-leading?"

"I'm acting alone. I would be surprised if anyone else knows my situation as anything but a preference for staying inside the grounds." Her watchful gaze came up. "As I say, it would damage their memory of your grandmother if staff began gossiping. I'd rather you didn't make serious inquiries."

"You know as well as I do that without a thorough investigation, it's very much *she said, no one else said*. I've weathered disgruntled employees making wild accusations many times. I'm not concerned." He was a little concerned. This woman was not like the others here, that much was obvious. Not just in looks and background, either. At twenty-two, she had inveigled her way into controlling an elderly woman's fortune. She was infinitely more dangerous than she looked.

Luli's cheeks drew in as she set her chin. "Whether the police believe me or not, I expect they will deport me, seeing as I have no legal right to be here. My prospects in Venezuela are dim. I've had to make arrangements for that possibility."

"I bet you have." He couldn't recall the last person to be so bold in their stalk of his money. He was reluctantly fascinated. "Stealing is a crime."

"Only if I collect it."

"Indeed." He picked up his cup to sip and allow that lethal threat to sink in.

She might have paled slightly, but the sun had set and the light was changing.

"You could kill me," she acknowledged. "Or I could simply disappear. Contingencies have been prepared for that possibility, as well. The investigation into that would be very thorough and go on a very long time."

"Hell hath no fury like a woman with a keyboard. What did I do to deserve this wrath?"

Her hands, so prettily arranged in her lap, turned their palms up in a subtle entreaty. "I'm aware that my only value right now is my ability to reverse the inconveniences I've arranged."

"I'm confident I can reverse them myself before they do too much damage. Your value is nil."

"You're probably right." She nodded, not even sweating. Her only betrayal of nerves was the rapid tattoo of the artery in her throat.

Gabriel had a weakness for puzzles. There was a twelve-year-old boy inside him itching to lock the door, put on his noise-canceling headphones and hack his own system until he'd found every Easter egg she'd hidden there. Not because he was worried. Purely for the game of it.

And there was a thirty-one-year-old man who wanted to put his hands on the twisted pieces of this woman and see how quickly he could untangle her and make her come apart.

"If what you say about your circumstance here is true…" He set aside his coffee mug again. "One could argue that by taking control of my grandmother's assets, I am taking possession of you."

There was that intriguing stillness again. The screen of her mink lashes, so ridiculously long and curled like a filly's, hid her eyes while her mouth might have trembled.

"One could argue that," she admitted in a voice that wasn't quite steady. "I've done my utmost to protect all of her assets. Including me. Which wouldn't stop you from unloading me. As assets go, I'm probably at my top value right now. If you were to sell me, for instance."

He told himself she was mistaking him for someone with a conscience that could be played upon, but his stomach clenched in revulsion.

"Of course, if you were to do that, I would make every effort to use what I know of her business interests to my advantage," Luli continued.

Such a cool delivery. He told himself to focus on that, her complete lack of emotional hysteria despite the topic they were discussing.

Instead, he was compelled to ask, "Is that how she acquired you? Off some auction block?" He would turn the fortune over to the authorities, not wanting a penny of it if it was built on something so ugly.

"No." She shifted the fit of her hands, interlacing her fingers, but her knuckles remained white, telling him she was in a state of heightened stress, even though that was the only visible sign of it. Why? Because her story was true? Or because the lie she was telling had grown too heavy and unwieldy to carry?

"My mother lived in a building my father owned in Caracas. She was his mistress. He was in government, married to someone else. He sold the building to your grandmother without making arrangements for my mother's upkeep. Mae was trying to have her thrown out. My mother cut a deal with her to take me as an employee in exchange for allowing her to stay there. I'm working off my mother's debt."

She named a figure in bolivars that would calculate to about a hundred thousand dollars.

Was that what a human life was worth? Pocket change?

"You were fourteen?"

"Yes."

"Why haven't you left? Even if she deducted room and board, I would think you'd have paid that off by now."

"Where would I go?" Her hands came up empty. "If your grandmother has my passport, it's long expired. I have no right to be here and there's nothing for me in Venezuela if they deport me. I could live on the streets, I suppose, and work under the table as other illegals do. How is that better than this? At least here I'm safe, fed and clothed."

And now that safety net was gone. He began to understand her motive.

"I'm grateful to your grandmother," she continued. "I didn't fully understand it at the time, but there was a man who had also come to the apartment. If Mae hadn't insisted on taking me, I'm quite sure my mother would have given me to him. My computer work these last years would have been purely as content." Her faint smile was an inscrutable *Mona Lisa* of agonized acceptance.

No. A sharp spike of repugnance slid deep into his gut at the idea of any woman being exploited that way. At fourteen. *Ever.*

"She really doesn't pay you?"

"Please don't be offended when I say this."

She angled her head with apology. "I think she looked on me as a sort of daughter. She didn't pay me because you don't pay family for working in the family business."

"If that's how she saw you, why didn't she leave everything to *you*?"

"She said..." Luli sighed toward the ceiling. "She said that when the time was right, she would arrange a marriage for me. I don't know if she was serious, but if I brought up money, she would get defensive and ask me if I would be happier scrubbing pots in the kitchen."

"No one else knows about this agreement?" Could it be called an agreement if Luli hadn't been given a choice?

"I've never told anyone. I don't believe she ever did."

Because, no matter the lofty motives she might have had, holding Luli here like this was a crime.

Or a complete fabrication.

And his grandmother was gone. He couldn't ask her if she had really kept a young woman as an indentured servant for *eight years*.

"Mr. Dean—"

"Gabriel."

"Mr. Dean." Her voice made his scalp prickle, her accent so musical and warm despite her formal address. "I very much appreciate that you've given me this opportunity to explain myself." Her gaze slid to the clock on the mantel, an ornate bronze piece atop a trumpeting elephant, likely from one of the Louis periods.

"If you're willing to continue this conversation, I would like to reset the timer on the laptop."

He was impossible to read. Intimidating with his innate physical power on top of his wealth and influence. She had to continually remind herself to breathe. Inhale, exhale. No sudden movements. Predators were attracted by panic and the stench of fear.

She suspected he deliberately let the seconds tick audibly in the silent room as a small form of torture to her. A test, perhaps, to see how nervous it made her.

Poise was something she had begun cultivating as soon as she understood the word. She made herself hold his gaze, refusing to give up her small advantage until he agreed to her condition. If he thought what she had told him about herself was a complete fabrication, they would discover the hard way that it was true.

His head jerked in an abbreviated nod.

In a smooth, unhurried motion that hid the gallop of her heart, she went to the desk and opened the laptop with a single minute to spare. She used the opportunity of having her back turned to gather her composure. Her fingerprint unlocked the screen, but she had to enter a code at the same time and she had to get it right in two tries. She managed it, then navigated to give them another thirty minutes of playing chess on a minefield.

As she turned, she found him on his feet. He removed his suit jacket and draped it over the arm of the sofa. His shirt strained across the virile expanse of his shoulders and chest and tucked into the narrow belt to accentuate his lean waist.

"More *kopi*?" She moved to the tray where the urn sat, more to avoid approaching him than a desire to be a conscientious servant.

He brought his cup to the tray. "No, thank you."

A deliberate effort to approach *her*? His jawline was what some might refer to as chiseled. It was a clearly defined, angular structure from corner to corner, quite a fascinating study for an artist's eye.

Or the eye of a woman who'd spent her adolescence in something like a harem, surrounded by women and a few off-limits middle-aged men.

Gabriel's chin went up a degree so his narrow eyes looked down his straight nose at her. "How much do you want?"

She dropped her hands to the sides of her dress, palms gently cupped, fingers pointed, but relaxed. *No fidgeting.*

"This isn't blackmail."

"If it looks like blackmail and smells like blackmail..." he scoffed darkly.

"I don't want it to be," she clarified, making herself hold her ground despite the twitches of alarm pulsing in her limbs. "I've had ample opportunities to steal. I enjoy this position of trust with your grandmother because I've never betrayed her. I've worked for her in good faith, not to repay my mother's debt, but to thank her for removing me from my mother's power."

"And you no longer owe her that allegiance?"

"I don't owe it to you."

His expression didn't change, but the scent of danger stung her nostrils, making her want to skitter away out of self-preservation.

"Not yet," she allowed, fighting to keep him from seeing how unsure and frightened she really was.

"Oh, might I earn the privilege of your holding *my* fortune for ransom? Do tell me how."

That was sarcasm. She could tell.

Saying nothing, she took refuge in her long-ago training, tucked her heel into the arch of her other foot and squared her shoulders. A smile of any kind was beyond her in this moment, but she kept her expression relaxed, stood tall with a long neck. She tucked in her butt and did her best to project self-assurance and limitless patience.

"What kind of person are you, Luli of the deceitful intelligence?" He sounded scathing, but as his gaze swept down, she thought it caught on her chest, lingered.

She became aware of the weight of cotton across the swells of her breasts. A prickly, heavy sensation made her ultraconscious that she *had* breasts. A tight, pinched sensation hit her nipples, making heat flush from the pit of her stomach up to her cheeks for no reason at all.

When his gaze came back to hers, something flickered in his expression. Curiosity and something avid. Luli had known about him for years and had studied him online in the same way she read facts about bears and deadly vipers, without quite believing such a creature existed because she'd never seen one with her own eyes. Even so, she knew she ought to be terrified if she ever came face-to-face with one.

She was terrified.

But she continued to stand there. Had to. She held her ground because she had no other options.

"I propose that I work for you in the same capacity as I have for your grandmother."

"Free?"

"More or less." She cleared the strain from her throat. She had known this would be a tough sell, given the anvil she had positioned over all that he was poised to inherit. "I would assist in the transition at no cost to you in exchange for other considerations."

"I have no reason to trust you. Clean up your mess—" He nodded at the laptop. "—and your debt to my grandmother is zero. You'll be free to go."

The floor seemed to fall away from beneath her.

"Where?" She carefully modulated her tone so her fear of abandonment wasn't obvious. "I have no money. If I wanted to live as a refugee, I would have run away years ago." She was so *tired* of being powerless. Of feeling as though she owed her very existence to someone else.

"You want to stay here?" He folded his arms, signaling his refusal. "No. I *will* take control of her fortune, if only to knock your fingers off it. You are no longer needed, Luli."

"*I know that.* Why do you think I'm doing this?" It came out with the fervent anger she had sublimated for years, emotions flaring so hot, her eyes burned.

"What do you want then?"

The things she wanted were so far out of reach, she had stopped thinking about them long ago. Love, security, a place where she belonged…those were luxuries. She had to focus on what she *needed*—a means to support herself.

"I want to move to one of the modeling capitals. New York, preferably."

"You want to be a model?" He said it with such disparagement, she let her weight shift onto her back foot.

"You don't think I'm pretty enough?" Panic edged in from all sides. This was all she had!

"Why haven't you done it already? Singapore has a thriving fashion district."

"Of Asian models. My look doesn't fit this market. It's not a profession where you walk in a door and get a job anyway. You have to build up to it, provide headshots and find an agent."

He waved at the laptop. "You have options. Why haven't you made inroads?" He sounded incredulous.

"Your grandmother couldn't run her business without me. Not the way she liked to run it." Her conscience grew heavy with the familial obligation she had alluded to a few minutes ago. "And she would never have forgiven me. She was furious with your mother for leaving without her permission."

The sudden flash in his eyes told her that particular topic was off-limits.

She resisted the urge to tangle her hands together and wring them.

"I've been struggling these last few years, aware that she needed me, but also aware that the two advantages I possess—youth and looks—won't be available to me forever. If I'm going to exploit them, it has to be now."

"Don't overlook that cunning brain of yours."

"Much as I would prefer to be valued for my intellect, who will hire someone without accreditation or even a home and a computer of her own? The work I do for your grandmother isn't transferable to anyone except you. And my use to you has a very short shelf life. *I know that.*"

She sighed, trying to keep hold of her composure as she continued.

"Her passing has forced me to secure my future as quickly and expediently as possible. Models with the right look can work anywhere. They're paid well and agencies help with the travel and residency paperwork."

"You just pointed out that no one walks into that career."

"It depends who escorts me, doesn't it?" She was way out on her wobbly limb now, grip slipping and the whole tree swaying in hurricane-force wind.

His brows went up. She'd watched those raptor wings lift like that several times, expressing his astonishment at the audacious mouse in his sharp-taloned foot, chittering no matter how hard he squeezed her.

He smiled faintly. "I wondered when we were going to get to an offer like that."

The tip of his finger grazed her temple in a caress that tucked a stray hair behind her ear.

Any further words she might have found became tangled in her throat because his fingertip continued that nascent caress into the hollow beneath her ear, then stroked the soft flesh beneath her jawbone, tilting up her chin before she had realized she was obeying his silent command.

"Pleasant as that inducement promises to be..." His voice grated sensually across her nerve endings. "I won't be persuaded to let you handle my grandmother's money. Or me."

He dropped his touch, sending a chill through her whole body.

Dragging his gaze off the temptation of her plump, shiny, parted lips took every ounce of Gabriel's well-honed discipline. He controlled all that he did because he controlled *himself.* Giving in to impulse, especially the sexual kind, was juvenile.

But the flare of yearning and disappointment in his eyes was almost his undoing.

"I wasn't...um...trying to offer s-sex for—"

"The stutter is a nice touch. Most men go crazy for the helpless damsel act. Good on you for trying it." It was her first show of vulnerability amid a nerves-of-steel performance. He wasn't buying it, though. "I'm impervious."

Mostly. His hands itched to drag her against his chest, not only because he wanted to do things to her—carnal, wicked things—but because the tremble in her lashes tugged at something in him. Against his better judgment, he felt an urge to shelter her. Reassure her.

She didn't argue or stammer out more protestations. There might have been a glimmer of injury behind her eyes, but it was gone so quickly, he knew it was only a strategy that was briefly considered before she discarded it. Within seconds, she returned to her true, iron-butterfly persona.

"Sex is firmly off the table?" Her tone gave him the sense he was missing something.

"I never force sex and I never pay for it. I am, however, open to enjoying it anywhere, including on tables."

"I'm willing to offer other acts that might be of value to you, then. Marriage, for instance."

"You want me to marry you? I honestly didn't think you could astound me further. Not my first offer. Thank you, but no." He rejected her firmly even as a voice in the back of his brain reminded that he would have to begin thinking of marriage. Was he going to leave his fortune to those idiot cousins of his father's?

He brushed that aside, needing all his concentration to deal with this surprisingly daring and skillful con woman. Especially when she seemed genuinely taken aback by his words.

"I don't want to marry *you*. You're far too young," she said, as if the idea was ridiculous.

"I stand corrected," he drawled. "I am further astounded."

"I would make an excellent trophy wife. I'm open to considering marriage to a man of advanced years at your direction, provided I'm granted residency in a major center like New York or London."

"You want to marry someone twice your age?"

"Three at least." She frowned. "I'm only twenty-two."

"Now you're trying too hard." He couldn't help it. He laughed openly.

"Marrying an older man worked out well for your grandmother. She was widowed at thirty."

"They say emulation is the sincerest form of flattery." He folded his arms. "But I am not a pimp. Old men may find their trophy wives without my assistance." The idea of lecherous, gnarled hands claiming those curves revolted him to the point of violent rage.

She looked to the window. There might have been a sheen on her eyes and a pout in her lips as she ran out of gambits, but he felt no triumph. He was captivated by the sheer perfection in her exquisite profile, graceful as a cameo carved into ivory.

She was so remote and untouchable in that moment, his abdomen clenched with craving for something he couldn't articulate.

"Very well." She moved to the laptop and glanced at him. "I'll undo everything I've done if I have your word it will square my debt with your grandmother and I'll be free to go. No police."

He heard the defeat in her tone and experienced loss, even though he had won. He wasn't ready for this game to end, but he made himself nod agreement.

She touched the tip of her finger to the sensor.

"Just to be clear..." She slanted a glance at him.

Foreboding filled him—and thrill. He had thought she was giving up, but this delightfully tricky wench didn't seem to know the meaning of the word *quit*.

"Yes?" he asked with deliberate lack of concern that bordered on tedium.

"When I say *everything*..."

"That doesn't exactly clean up your mess, does it?" He let fury lick at him because it was better than allowing her magnificence to blind him.

"If Luli isn't needed, everything under that profile must also be unnecessary," she said with simple logic.

"Come here."

She stayed where she was, but had the good sense to take her hands off the laptop and close the screen.

"Do you realize how dangerous I am?"

"Do you realize," she asked in an even quieter voice, lips white, "how little I have to lose? How much I've already lost?"

Eight years, if she was to be believed.

Her hands were curled into angry fists, but stayed at her sides. "You're welcome, by the way, for all the times I've asked your grandmother, *Is this an opportunity you would like me to bring to your grandson's attention?* You could have stepped in at any time to help her manage her affairs. You didn't. *I* did. For nothing but a roof over my head and three meals a day."

"And you think you can strike back at *me* for that? By deleting a few paper trails? Any database or personnel records you compromise can be rebuilt from backups. It won't take long and the price tag won't be that high."

"I estimate the cost at ten million US dollars, based on penalties for failing to finalize certain contracts on time. Or you could keep me on and not lose a penny."

"Is that what you think you're worth?" he scoffed. "Ten million dollars?"

His words pushed a pin in her back, forcing her to take a step toward him. Anger smoldered around her in a cloud, making her entirely too sexy and distracting when her voice was so sharp and profound.

"I've spent years thinking my value is less than zero. I thought I had to stay here because Mae was the only person who wanted me, and only if I was useful to her. From the moment I emailed you that she had collapsed, my only thought has been that I have to prove my worth to you, but how do I do that when I'm a walking, unpaid debt?" Her hand moved to press into her middle, as though clutching at a knife stuck in her navel. "The debt is my mother's. I am worth exactly what *I* decide I'm worth. If I'm to be exploited, *I* will choose the terms. And if you're going to put me on the street like a stray dog, you *will* feel the bite of it."

A discreet knock on the door had him snapping out, "Busy!"

An older brown-faced woman was already

peeking in. "I'm sorry, Mr. Dean. I was told you left instructions I report to you the minute I returned."

"Mrs. Chen's nurse," Luli said, stepping back and letting her hair fall forward to shield how color had risen in her face during their confrontation.

He swore under his breath and nodded at the woman. "Come in."

He swung back to Luli and pointed at her laptop. "Put that on hold for a few hours. Then tell the butler to prepare us dinner." He needed a damned minute to think.

The nurse bounced her gaze between the two of them as Luli moved to the desk and tapped a few keys. Seconds later, Luli closed the door behind her.

The nurse didn't give him any information he didn't already have. She offered condolences; he promised a severance package so she could take her time finding another position. She bowed slightly when he dismissed her.

"Wait," he said. "How long have you been with my grandmother?"

She turned back, expression brightening the way most of his employees did when he gave them the opportunity to prove their value to him.

"Almost twenty years, sir."

"You've known Luli since she came here? How long has she been working here in my grandmother's office?"

"From the beginning, sir."

"That was my grandmother's idea? Was she competent? My grandmother, I mean. Mentally."

"Oh, completely, sir! But Mrs. Chen never cared for telephones or computers." Her hand washed such things from the air. "She thought them unhealthy and brought Luli in as a convenience. Luli spoke Spanish and your grandmother had recently acquired properties in South America."

"Luli was quite young when she arrived? What was she like?" Scared? Angry?

"Quiet." The nurse's expression faltered as she delved into her memory.

"Because she only spoke Spanish?" He seldom thought about his teen years, but recalled adolescent girls traveling in colorful flocks and relentlessly twittering at each other. No matter what the truth was today, Luli must have felt isolated at the time.

"She spoke a little English, but it was the patch that was the problem. I had to remove it from her tongue. I had completely forgotten about that," the nurse said with a distant frown.

"What kind of patch?" he asked sharply.

"For weight loss. It makes it painful to eat solids. She was already stick thin, but young women will do the stupidest things to themselves in the name of fashion. Mrs. Chen saved her from herself, if you want my opinion."

CHAPTER THREE

A CRISP RAP on her door snapped her awake.

Luli glanced at her alarm clock, but it wouldn't go off for another hour. She had set it so she wouldn't oversleep resetting the timer on the laptop.

"Luli," *he* said. "Open the door or I'm coming in."

She quickly rose and brushed her hands down her wrinkled dress, then opened the door to Gabriel's glower.

He glanced past her to the dented pillow on the single bed, the plain walls and utilitarian night table with only a clock and hairbrush upon it.

"What are you doing?" he demanded.

"Sleeping."

"You're supposed to be eating dinner with me. Why did you tell the butler I wanted to eat with *him*?"

"You said, *Tell the butler to prepare us dinner.* I presumed *us* meant him."

"No, you didn't," he said flatly.

It had been open for interpretation and she'd been dead on her feet. Also, there was no way the butler would believe the new master of the house wanted to eat with her unless he heard it directly from Gabriel himself. He and all the rest of the staff had given her apprehensive looks, everyone asking, *What did you tell him?*

And, exactly as she did when it came to her closed-door conversations with Mrs. Chen, she had given up nothing—earning zero friends in the process.

Now she'd made Gabriel angry. She'd fallen asleep thinking about his nearly kissing her, imagining things she barely understood. What would it feel like to have his lips on hers, his hand moving to her bottom? Her breasts. Between her legs.

Fresh heat pressed there, disconcerting her. How was it that all she had to do was think about him, stand before him, and quivers shook her abdomen and her mouth watered? It was mortifying.

"I'm not hungry," she tried in a voice that scraped.

"I'm not requesting."

His hard tone told her that all the work she'd put into giving herself leverage had left her with virtually none.

"Garden," he said, stepping back to indicate she should lead the way.

She did, self-conscious the entire time that he was right behind her. She arrived to find a table had been set with Mae's best china on a silk cloth. One of the maids brought the first course, a small bowl of curry *laksa* made with shrimp and cockles. Gabriel handled the vermicelli with his golden chopsticks as adeptly as she did.

And noticed the curious look she sent after the maid.

"I gave the butler the night off," he said. "After clarifying he wasn't my date."

"I'm sure he appreciates a free evening." He was going to kill her when he saw her next.

"He didn't offer many compliments when I asked him about you."

It didn't really surprise her that he'd made those inquiries, but it made her squirm inwardly, knowing that no one would have anything very nice to say. She never dwelt on her ache of loneliness, but it was humiliating to have the staff's contempt of her become the centerpiece of this already painful dinner.

"I sat in on his meetings with Mae when they reviewed household expenses and raises. It was my task to prepare the performance reviews and suggest appropriate wage increases."

His laugh was a single cut of disbelief. "Have you made *any* friends here?"

"Perhaps you'll be my first," she said with a smile of false hope.

She watched for a twitch of humor in his mouth, but it held its tense line while she only wound up thinking about his rejection of her perceived advances.

She lost her appetite and set aside her chopsticks.

"I read your note," he announced.

"Which—? Oh." She realized as she brought her gaze back up to his antagonized one.

He must have tried to hack his way into the network while she'd been sleeping. Of course he had. And he'd found her warning against proceeding further.

"I thought this whole thing a bluff, but those are an elegant few lines capable of doing *so much* damage. I have an idea how to get around it. I've cloned the entire thing to a testing file. I'll crack it before I go to bed," he said with confidence, nipping off the tail of a shrimp and setting it aside as he chewed the meat.

"You realize there's more?" she asked cautiously.

"I'd be disappointed if there wasn't." His smile was as false as hers had been. "Where did you learn to code?"

"We had to design our own website at school. There were a handful of standard templates to choose from. We were supposed to load basic details and a few photos, that kind of thing. I didn't like the colors it offered and wanted a different layout. I looked up how to hack into the back end and customize it."

"For extra credit?"

"To stand out from the rest. We were also required to have a hobby and volunteer hours. I chose programming and contributed to open-source projects. Since I've been here, I've had time and opportunity to become proficient in several languages. Mae liked that I could manipulate things to the way she wanted them."

"Coding is a skill that's very marketable," he pointed out.

"That's why I'm demonstrating my skills to you." She pushed her bowl away. "But who will take me seriously, without a track record or credentials? Which door do I knock on when I land after being deported and have nothing in my pockets but lint? At best, I'd be recruited for click farms or phishing scams, maybe have to resort to criminal activity for my own survival. As I said before, if I wanted to break laws, I would have already."

"You don't fit the stereotype for coding geeks—I'll give you that." His penetrating look made her want to touch her hair and see if it was falling out of its knot. He certainly was unraveling *her*.

The maid exchanged their soup for plates of barbecued stingray.

As Luli scraped a tiny morsel of meat from the wing and dabbed it in the sauce, Gabriel asked, "Are you concerned about your weight?"

"I don't care for seafood. And these portions were obviously meant for the butler."

"Order something else." He looked for the maid who had already carried their dirty bowls away.

"I don't see how acting too good for the chef's food will improve my social standing. It's fine. I like the chili sauce with the rice."

He tucked into his own. "The nurse said you were wearing a weight-loss patch on your tongue when you came here. Why?"

"For weight loss." He was not a man to be played with, she *knew* that, but she knew where this was going and would really rather not.

"*Why* did you want to lose weight?"

She bit back a sigh.

"Advantage. My mother requested the school attach it and I went along with it. Many girls had liposuction or nose jobs. The tongue patch was nothing." She dismissed it with a twitch of her shoulder.

"What kind of school would arrange such things?"

"One that trains pageant contestants."

"You were training for a beauty contest?"

She lifted her gaze, mildly affronted. "Why is that shocking? I was a front-runner."

"I didn't know there was such a thing. This is the same school where you were making websites?"

"To build our online presence from the earliest age, yes. I was eleven when I started and built it into something that would have been a decent calling card today, but it's long been taken down." She was still annoyed at her hard work disappearing into cyberspace.

"This is why you wanted your site to stand out from the crowd?"

"Everything was a contest." Understatement of the decade. She tasted another bite of stingray. It was smoky and stringy, but tender and not too fishy. Tolerable.

"Which means no friends there, either?" he guessed.

"Some girls were friendly, but my mother's view was that a consolation sash like Miss Congeniality is for those who need consoling—something winners don't require, so there was no need to aspire to achieve it. She once played a vicious mind game with a rival, though, by pretending she was trying to win that particular title."

"Your mother competed?"

"Won every major title, yes."

"And yet she had no money for an apartment?"

"She has expensive tastes. And she was angry with my father. Me, too, I think."

"Why?"

Luli sighed, hating to face this head-on.

"There's renown in keeping the crown in the family and the prize money I won paid for my school, but how can you claim to be the most beautiful woman in the world if your own daughter is threatening to take the title from you?"

"She sounds like a lovely person. Did no one notice you dropped out and disappeared?"

"She told people I'd gone to live with relatives. A few schoolmates inquired online and I backed her up. The reality was too…"

To this day, thinking of her mother's casual divesting of her sent a lightning strike of agony into her heart. Her mother had been purely self-serving. It was why she'd had an affair with a married man in the first place. Getting pregnant had probably been one more way to squeeze support out of him. One more thing she hadn't thought through and wound up regretting. She had considered her daughter a commodity and certainly never loved her the way mothers were supposed to love their children. It had left Luli with a gaping emptiness in her soul, one Mae hadn't filled, but had at least acknowledged and attempted to paper over.

"I wasn't sorry to be away from my mother," Luli admitted quietly. "I saw no point in telling people what had really happened. The best-case scenario would have been that she was arrested and I would be living as an orphan there, without prospects. Not even at school any longer."

"Did you want to compete? Or did she force you to do that, too?"

"I saw opportunity and applied myself. I only competed in national titles for girls in the younger categories. I left before I moved into the teen contests. I'm confident I would do well in the global pageants if I entered today. It's one of my contingency plans, if I'm deported. There's quite an investment up front, though. You have to win all the feeder pageants. It's a long game." She was talking too fast. "That's the only reason I set up an account for myself in Venezuela. If I'm forced to draw from it, I promise I'll pay you back with interest."

He didn't immediately refuse her, only narrowed his eyes. "Pageants sound like a path to modeling. Would it be so bad to start there?"

"In Venezuela? The minute I gained any sort of publicity, my mother would come back into my life. I'd prefer to avoid that."

"That's the main reason you don't want to be deported? Your mother?"

"*Sí.*" She poked at the stingray flesh, unable to take another bite of it.

"Stop torturing that. It's already dead." He took her barely touched plate and set it atop his emptied one. "I'll finish it if you're only going to play with it."

"I'll clean toilets if that becomes the only option available to me," she told him, clutching her empty hands in her lap. "I *will* pursue programming, which I know can pay well, but it's also a long game. My physical attributes mean I can aim for a higher and faster return if I try modeling or something like it. It only makes sense that I try. Don't you agree?"

She held her breath, waiting for his assessment. So far he hadn't pulled any punches. If he said she wasn't attractive enough, she would rethink her strategy.

His gaze swept across her face in an almost tangible caress, like a cool scarf of silk wafted over her skin.

"I can't deny you're beautiful." The gravel in his tone had her reflexively holding her breath, waiting for a strange all-over ache to subside.

Then he looked away and his expression hardened, making something catch in her chest. She wanted him to keep looking at her, keep sending that electric current through her that held such possibility.

"I'm only asking that you take me with you and give me time to establish myself," she pleaded softly. "I'll continue my work on Mae's investments in exchange for accommodation and meals—"

"Quite the bargain, considering your minimalist approach to both."

"I would need a small loan for clothing and

makeup, but I can continue wearing this uniform for office work—"

"Like hell you can."

She closed her eyes, angry with herself for
trying too hard. Judges could always smell
desperation.

Ignoring the sting behind her eyes, she
considered other avenues of persuasion. He
hadn't seemed interested in sex in exchange
for favors, maybe because he sensed her inexperience in that department? Should she
tell him she'd read up on that particular topic?
Extensively? She was always willing to put
in the work to do better.

Soft footsteps sounded. The maid arrived
with braised duck on a bed of colorful, juli-
enned vegetables.

"Take that one back," he said of Luli's plate
before the maid could set it. "You enjoy it.
We'll share this one. I'm getting full." He sent
Luli a droll look as he set the single plate between them.

The maid curtsied and hurried away with
her full plate and fresh gossip. Luli imagined
she would be accused of sleeping with Mrs.
Chen's grandson very soon. Little did they
know he had already turned her down.

"Mr. Dean—"

He dipped his chin in warning.

"Gabriel?" She said it softly, not wanting to be overheard when it felt so much like an overstep. She was still the youngest on staff and always addressed others formally or at least with a respectful *auntie*.

"Eat," he commanded. "My turn to talk."

He was the one who had asked so many questions, forcing her to go on and on. She singled out a pale stick of daikon and nibbled the sweet-spicy end of it.

He sat back and regarded her with flinty eyes as he sipped his wine.

"You accused me of neglecting my grandmother—not stepping in to manage things before today. She disowned my mother before I was born. I met Mae for the first time at my mother's funeral when I was seven. I didn't see her again until five years had passed. My father warned me about allowing her to influence me, which seemed paranoid, but he knew her better than I did. I saw her again at my father's funeral and we remained in touch—through you, I now realize, but I never made assumptions about whether I would inherit her fortune. As for assisting in managing her wealth... How would I know she needed help? You've done your job so well, I had no cause for concern."

Was that a compliment or a rebuke?

He set down his stemless glass.

"I, however, have no need for your management services. Chen Enterprises is mine. I'll chew and swallow it the way I would any other company that falls under my control, restructuring where necessary and allowing my existing legion of executives to do what I pay them to do."

She kept her expression a stiff mask, not revealing the crumple inside her.

"As to the threats you've made, my life is completely impervious to them. I don't need my grandmother's money and her misdeeds are not mine. I'm not close enough to her for her loss of good standing to affect my pride. You're the one who will feel it if you implode her legacy. I'll walk away unscathed."

She had known that, deep down. She had known she had no real leverage. She had nothing and was nothing. Her throat tightened and it took all her effort to keep the press of tears from reaching the front of her eyes.

"So I'm to be deported?" Her stomach fell while the flutter of nerves behind her heart became the panicked batter of bird wings against a window.

He wasn't saying anything.

Through the lashes she dropped to disguise

her agony, she saw his lips curl, but it wasn't a smile. Self-deprecation, perhaps.

She set down her chopsticks, but she couldn't think beyond that.

"You're not going to eat? Come with me, then." He rose abruptly and started into the house.

She half expected to be shown the front door, but he went up the wide staircase and strode into Mae's bedroom. She trailed him on feet that felt encased in cement, heart dragging as a weight behind her.

She had only been in this bedroom a handful of times. It was the purview of Mae's personal maid and her nurse, decorated in Mae's signature classic style without too much fuss or femininity, if a little dated. Mae never spent money unless she had to.

The mirror over the makeup table swung open like a cupboard. Gabriel revealed a safe and punched in the code.

"How did you—?"

"You can open these older safes by setting them back to their factory default. It takes longer to look up the combination online than it does to actually break in." He removed a leather-bound portfolio. "I was looking for her will and also I found this." He handed the portfolio to her.

"What is it?" She unzipped it to see a handful of her standard reports on some Chinese businessmen. Head shots, the natures of their businesses, net worth, any red flags that might cause Mae to have concerns about partnering with them.

"I don't know why she had this in her safe. It's a very typical—" She flipped past the third profile and found a document that read Marriage Contract.

"Oh, my God!" She threw it all away so the pages and photographs and colored notes with Mae's spidery handwriting fluttered like a flock of startled birds, then drifted to the silk rug to leave a jagged, broken puzzle upon it.

"Why so surprised? You said she was arranging you a marriage," he chided.

"I didn't know she was *doing* it!"

She hugged herself, staring in morbid horror at the papers. What did they say? What had Mae hoped to get in exchange for her? What was she worth *this* time?

"The dowry she was offering was quite generous. There's a decent settlement if you divorce, especially if you stick it out at least five years. Excellent terms if you provide children, especially sons."

"*When?* I thought—" She had thought Mae

wanted her. That she was doing a good job for her.

She had told him what she was, but it was pure debasement to stand here before him, proven to be nothing but an asset to be bartered in one more business deal. Chattel.

"The one in textiles is the oldest. Has a heart condition."

Luli turned her head, expression persecuted.

Gabriel's conscience twinged, but he was still processing this discovery himself. He had removed the folder with his name on it, curious to see if she would betray a notice of its absence.

She seemed genuinely shocked by the existence of this portfolio at all. The fact it had been stored in the safe told him Mae had wanted to keep it very private. Her notes on each of the candidates revealed explicitly how she saw each of those older men falling short in her estimation, especially as compared to *him*.

That had been the most disturbing discovery. These other men were fallback positions. Mae had wanted *him* as Luli's husband.

Because she did, in fact, seem to view Luli as a daughter. His efforts to find Luli on any payroll list or other household record had turned up nothing. He had personally questioned the butler who had shown him his own system for tracking staff hours and vacation days, but Luli wasn't on it.

She had her own arrangement, the butler had said with affront. And no, she didn't leave the house, which was a nuisance. Other staff had to pick up her personal items and the cost went against his household budget—a perk not available to anyone else. In his opinion, if staffing cuts were needed, Gabriel should start with Luli.

Gabriel remembered clearly the feeling of his own money, earned honestly and through great effort, going to support his father. It wasn't something he should resent. As Luli had said earlier, family supported family, but his father had abandoned any effort to do his part. It had all fallen on Gabriel at a very young age to keep him and his father clothed, sheltered and fed.

Luli had to be suffering a similar impotent anger. She had put in the time, had done what was expected, but that work had gone unacknowledged. Her reward was the opportunity to do the same for a stranger. Him or some other man.

"I won't do it." Her voice shook with the

rest of her. She lifted her gaze from staring through sheened eyes at the pages she'd thrown across the floor. "You can't make me."

"Calm down. I'm only saying that I'll honor her intentions if you want to go through with it." He was testing her, was what he was doing.

"Of course I don't!" She covered her face, visibly trying to take hold of herself.

"You said you would make a good trophy wife. That's what this is." He had never aspired to have any sort of wife—trophy or otherwise. That Mae had thought she could interfere in his life to this degree was a shocking affront.

"I want to marry on *my* terms," Luli said, echoing his own sentiments. She dropped her hands to reveal a raw agony in her expression that made his heart lurch. "I thought she *liked* me. Why would she do this?"

He had his theories, but asked instead, "Was there any indication she was ill? Was she putting things in order because she thought her time was near?"

"I don't think so." She paced a few steps, calming a little as she thought. "She only brought it up a few times. One of the maids left to get married last year. Mae said I wouldn't have to marry some fish-smelling man from the hawker center. She said she'd find me a good husband. But she also told me at different times that she would take me shopping and let the chauffeur teach me to drive and take me back to Venezuela so I could tell my mother what I think of her. It was never a good time for any of those things. 'Another day,'" she tacked on in Mandarin.

Presumably she was quoting Mae. Her accent was spot-on.

"I don't think she was lying to me on purpose," she continued despondently. "She talked about a lot of things that never happened. She wanted to redecorate. Retire. She said when you came to visit we would take you to see the sights."

Gabriel had seen the ones he wanted to see. He'd been here several times and had never once let his grandmother know he was in town.

His stomach tightened in disgust with himself. Had she meant to introduce him to Luli? Oversee their courtship?

So what if she had? What he'd said earlier about having no interest in finding women for other men stood. He had no desire for his dead grandmother to find him a wife, either.

But he ruefully had to admit she had never led him astray with any of the other opportunities she had presented to him.

"I don't want to marry one of those men and be trapped here for the rest of my life." Luli's hushed voice made something grate in the base of his throat. "Why would she do that to me?"

Why had Mae thought she could do this to him? The answer was the same in both cases.

"She was angry my mother didn't abide by the marriage she wanted for her. Good children allow their parents to make them a good match."

"I'm not her child and I'm not doing it!"

He held up a hand. "But this does prove she saw you as a foster daughter. She was taking a personal interest in your future the way she thought a mother should. She wasn't finding husbands for any of the housemaids. Only you."

In fact, like the rest of the house staff, the maids were entitled to a settlement based on their years of service. Gabriel had shown that part of Mae's will to the butler and told him to begin making plans to take the house down to a skeleton staff.

Luli wasn't house staff, though. Not that it

mattered. Gabriel could offer her any amount that he deemed fair out of his own pocket and ignore his grandmother's wishes. He owed Mae nothing.

Except that she had birthed the woman who had given him life. Luli could tell him things about his grandmother, maybe even his mother, that likely no one else could.

He cursed silently and ran a hand through his hair.

"I don't know how to *ask* to be deported." Luli moved to the window where she stared down at the courtyard. Her shoulders seemed very narrow, all of her quite fragile despite her willowy height. "I'm worried they'll put me in jail if I admit I've been here all this time. I can't stay, though. I don't want to and I have nothing to stay for. I have no one to put in a good word to help me get a job or find a place to live. They all hate me for never doing laundry or dusting. They think I'm a freeloader."

Her fingers were digging in to her upper arms, liable to leave bruises beneath her smooth skin.

"I heard men on the other side of the garden wall talking about fake passports once. I should have called out to them, but I was afraid. They were talking about guns and drugs. I would have had to steal money from Mae's purse. They might have decided to come in if they realized—"

"Luli." The other suitors crumpled beneath his feet as he walked across to her. "My grandmother intended you would be looked after. That's proof of it." He pointed back to the billionaires found to be not quite good enough for Mae's surrogate daughter.

"She wanted to hand me to a stranger like I'm a…a thing." Her eyes were bright and angry.

"I don't think that's true." He had taunted her earlier that she was one more asset he was inheriting, though. And he might not need this inheritance from Mae, but if he intended to accept it, he had to take all of it—including the treasure she had confined to this house like an heirloom jewel tucked in a safe.

He took in Luli's ugly dress and flat-footed sandals, her hair rolled into a cinnamon bun at her nape, her hands like rocks in the wide, patch pockets of her dress.

Whatever *she* was, Mae had kept her close for a reason. She had valued Luli highly enough to think her good enough for her only grandson. For that reason alone, he couldn't throw Luli away. Not without a thorough polish and appraisal first, he deduced with dark humor.

"You'll honor the dowry if I marry one of them?" she asked with dread, glancing at the papers with desperation and anguish.

Repulsion gripped him as he thought again of gnarled hands setting themselves against those luscious curves. If anyone touched her, he wanted it to be *him*.

"No. I want you to marry *me*."

flipped past the summary of his holdings and showed her the contract with their names already written into it.

Her sharp inhale told him that had been a blow she hadn't expected. He'd been shocked, too. And had wanted to see her reaction, to be sure she hadn't set this up. Her lips were white, her pupils tiny dots.

"You don't want to marry me! Do you?" she asked with trepidation.

"Marriage has not been a priority for me," he admitted, but frowned.

Mae was the only person he had ever listed as his beneficiary because she was the closest relative he had. There were reasons he hadn't pursued marriage and children, one of them being that he would have to wade through a swamp of gold diggers to find someone suitable.

Regardless of how uncomfortable it made him that Mae had plotted like this, there was something very expedient and businesslike in having marriage and progeny sourced and negotiated so all he had to do was agree to the terms. It provided a beautifully simple means of keeping emotions out of the equation.

"You could just give me the dowry," Luli urged with faint hope.

If everything she had told him was true—

CHAPTER FOUR

"What?" Her eyes went round as big blue plates. "Why? *No.*"

"It's what she wanted." He moved back to the safe and brought out the pages he'd removed from the portfolio, the one with his own head shot atop it. "I was in there, too."

"No." She shook her head and spoke in a hurried, half-panicked tone. "She often asked me to include you as a comparison when I prepared reports like this. She regarded you very highly, always measuring other businessmen by the standards you set."

"She asked me nine different times in the last year to come visit. How many times were any of those men invited here?"

"They live in the city. She didn't like to travel. She probably wanted you to come so she could tell you she was leaving everything to you."

"She wanted me to meet you. Look." He

and he was beginning to think it was—then she was too inexperienced to strike out alone, especially in a major center like New York or Paris, money in her pockets or not. The idea of her disappearing into thin air didn't sit well.

"It's very likely Mae intended to make our marriage a condition of my inheriting." He likely would have refused, but now he'd met Luli and wasn't so sure. He saw so much untapped potential in her. "In the same way I'm honoring her arrangements for the staff, I should provide you what she intended you to have."

"A husband? Lucky me," she choked.

He was both amused and insulted.

"This is a very quick means of gaining you residency in New York, where you said you wanted to go. I'd prefer to get back there without delay." He handed her the contract. "Read it. If you agree it's favorable, we'll sign it in the morning, marry and be on our way."

"New York? Really?" For the first time, an avid flash glittered in her eyes.

It made him cautious enough to add, "And this way I can be sure you're not embezzling to accounts in South America or dropping inconvenient PR bombshells."

She rolled the contract and held it in her

fist, cocked her head in suspicion. "Am I supposed to disable everything now?"

"This isn't a trick." He hid a smile at how much he enjoyed the way she held ground and presented a challenge at every turn. "Disable the timer. I'll break in on my own time and assess what you've done. I don't like that you've found vulnerabilities. I'll examine those doors and seal them myself, ensure nothing like this can happen again."

Maybe this was the real attraction to marrying her, he mused as she frowned and left the room. He wanted to delve past her defenses and understand how *she* worked.

It was an opportunity that felt too good to turn down. And Luli had run out of options. Losing Mae had left her bereft in many ways.

The marriage contract *was* quite generous, but he didn't really want to give her an allowance, did he? Not that much? She crossed it out and set a question mark beside it for discussion. What about the settlements for children? Did he expect them to have sex? Or was this a marriage in name only?

She went down early the next morning, wanting to talk it out, but he was much in demand. Solicitors and other officials were literally queued up, waiting their turn while he signed papers, made arrangements for Mae's cremation and held a small press conference.

She finally caught his eye by hovering in the doorway as he was dismissing someone.

"Ready?" he asked, waving her in with a frown at what she was wearing.

He had asked her to put on something for travel, but she didn't own anything except her uniform dresses. She had stolen into Mae's closet for the only clothes that fit her wide hips and ample chest. The pleated skirt was a mustard color, the brocade jacket double-breasted and so dated it had mattresses for shoulder pads.

She smiled a hesitant greeting at Mae's lawyer who sat with a clerk on the sofa, papers laid out before them on the coffee table. Another man rose as she entered.

Gabriel took the pages from her, reading as he said, "Close the door. This is Mr. Johnson from the American embassy. He's liaising with the Venezuelan authorities to obtain your emergency passport and issue your permit to enter the US."

"Oh. Thank you. Nice to meet you." She shook the American's hand.

"I understand you're both very much in love," Mr. Johnson said, making a facetious V with his lips.

"What…?"

"He's officiating our marriage." Gabriel leaned on the desk to affix his signature to the bottom of the contract in a firm scratch. He offered the pen to her. "Which is, of course, a love match and not a work-around for residency."

She opened her mouth, wanting to say she had come in here to discuss the contract, not sign it. Not *do* this.

But there was Mr. Johnson, waiting to issue her a passport and the right to enter the US. All she had to do was keep her mouth shut.

She pressed her lips tight and took the pen in fingers that felt nerveless and clumsy. Her scrawl was jerky and not the least bit pretty. In fact, she couldn't recall the last time she had written her whole given name.

Gabriel handed the document to the attorney then looked to Mr. Johnson.

Right there in front of Mae's desk, where Luli had stood a thousand times, she spoke vows to create a life with Gabriel, then signed another piece of paper and was pronounced his wife.

"You may kiss," Mr. Johnson said.

Gabriel was suddenly very close. Bigger. His eyes seeming to turn a dark, hunter green.

He was asking her a silent question, one she couldn't interpret, let alone answer.

The heat of his palm settled against the side of her neck. The width of his chest blocked out the world while his head came down.

She had wondered about kissing. There had been one, a very long time ago. It had been wet and off-putting and—

Conscious thought disappeared as the smooth heat of his lips grazed hers, once, twice. It caused a buzzing sensation, almost ticklish. Maddening. She found herself pressing into her toes, rising so her mouth more firmly met his, soothing the crazed feeling and suddenly his lips were fully sealed over hers.

Surprise held them both still for one heartbeat. Then his mouth moved in a lazy, curious taste of hers, parting her lips with the movement. Fireworks detonated under her skin and exploded against her closed eyelids.

A gasp caught in her throat, but it was the shock of having so many sensations accost her. His faint taste of bitter, black *kopi*, the scent of his aftershave on his smooth cheek, the sweep of his tongue that somehow sent a wrecking ball into her middle and another into her pounding heart.

She splayed a hand over his chest. His

kiss grew more devouring. She found herself squeezed up against the solid wall of his chest. His hard arms felt strangely good, if overwhelming. She was barely aware of what she was doing, moving her mouth against his out of instinct. Her arms unfurled to twine around his neck and she let her weight rest more fully against him as a drugged lassitude kept her in this wonderful place. She wanted to do this forever, mouth sliding against mouth, easing slightly then coming back with a deeper hunger. It was glorious.

He lifted his head and a noise of loss caught in her throat. His hands moved to her upper arms and he set her back a step, expression smoothed to something unreadable. He turned his head to look at Mr. Johnson. "Thank you."

It was like a bucket of cold water. Her head was still swimming, but she figured out that their kiss had been for the benefit of their small audience, not something that had affected him the way it had affected her.

"Collect your things," he said. "We'll leave shortly."

She nodded dumbly, not looking at anyone. It was starting to hit her that she had placed her future into the hands of a man with far more power than her mother's strident urging for her to win prize money or Mae's dictatorial demands.

Gabriel was master of everything he touched, including her. She had used up all her bravado yesterday—and played every card she had. Since then, she had actually discarded and folded a few. She had deactivated most of her insurance policies and had no doubt he would be able to hack into his own system within days. Then what would she be? Useless again.

And once again in a foreign land without a friend in the world.

At least here, she had her feet planted. The moment she left, she would be at his mercy.

Maybe she should stay, she thought with a wild rush of cowardice, hand shaking as she pushed her few things into a bag. Then she stared at the paltry evidence of her life here. With force of habit, her hand went to the front of her skirt, but failed to find the patch pockets where she kept a smooth stone she had found in the garden years ago.

It was on the night table and she dropped it into the bag.

Would the fish miss her throwing a handful of crumbs into the pond each morning? Would anyone miss her once she left here?

Gabriel was at the front door, seeing the men out. She went along to Mae's office where she started to unplug the laptop, but checked first to see if he had made any progress breaking in.

Not that she could tell. She confirmed that this week's payroll figures had been entered by all the department heads, then double-checked them and ensured the balances were available to cover it before she hit the keys that finalized the process.

Then she clicked over to market numbers. The announcement about Mrs. Chen's hospitalization might have caused a sell-off if the news hadn't been accompanied by the identity of her surprise grandson taking over. *That* had caused a rush to buy into some of her ventures, sending their value jumping several points.

Eight years of hard work and Luli hadn't made anywhere near the profit for Mae that Gabriel had by the simple act of connecting his name to Mae's.

She touched the power button, shutting down in disgust.

"What are you doing?" The butler's accusatory tone made her jump.

"I—" Did she have a guilty conscience? Very much so. "I'm packing." She wrapped the power cord around her hand and dropped it into her bag.

"Not that, you're not!" He puffed up with indignation. "You take *nothing*." He came across and tried to grab her bag to see inside it.

She backed up a few steps, distancing herself from his aggression. "Gabe—Mr. Dean is taking me to New York." She couldn't bring herself to tell him they'd just gotten *married*. "I need the laptop to keep working."

"You don't *work*." He made it sound as if she'd never lifted a finger in her life. "Were you on your knees when he said you could go with him? *Slut*." He sounded like one of her preteen fellow contestants.

"If this is about last night, I'm *sorry*." He felt tricked she supposed. "I misunderstood about dinner."

"You're not sorry. You wanted to make me look foolish. You were always trying to be Mrs. Chen's little pet and now you want to be his. Out. Now." He grabbed her by the arm.

Luli squeaked out a noise, so shocked at his getting physical, it took her a moment to dig in her heels and struggle against his hold.

"Let me go!" she cried.

He did—in a whirl of movement so fast she wound up clutching her hand against the thick fabric of her jacket's lapel, trying to keep her heart from leaving her chest.

Gabriel stood before her instead of the butler, but he was bent over and the butler was flat on his back on the floor. Gabriel's hand was pressed to the man's throat, turning the older man dark red.

"*You* will leave," he told the butler, switching his grip to the front of the man's shirt and yanking him to his feet as he straightened. "*Now.*"

Swaying in shock, the butler clutched a protective hand to his wheezing throat and hurried from the room.

Gabriel shot his cuffs and adjusted his tie, eyes ashen as he stared at her. "We're leaving." He jerked his head for her to precede him.

Luli was still dressed like a seventy-year-old woman, but Gabriel didn't tell her to change. He just wanted away from this place.

He was furious over what had just happened. He had nearly killed the man—who was in his fifties and no match for Gabriel's deadly training. It hadn't even been self-defense. The butler had been rude and rough, but Gabriel didn't think his intention had been to physically hurt Luli, only to force her from the house.

Even so, a haze of bloodlust had blinded him. He had acted on instinct and was still disturbed by his brief loss of control. Why had he reacted so strongly? He would intervene in any situation where someone was being bullied, but he wouldn't commit *homicide*.

The primal male in him had been roused by a threat to his mate, was the problem. His ears were still ringing from their kiss. He had meant to keep it a chaste peck, but her lips had been so soft. He had lingered, enjoying the tremulous way her mouth flowered open against his. Nothing had prepared him for the impact when she pressed into the kiss. A bolt of pure lust had jabbed through him, tightening his arms around her.

The rush of blood when her soft curves had collided with his frame had left his groin throbbing with the beat of his heart. It had been all he could do to set her back from him and keep an impassive look on his face when he'd wanted to snarl at the men to leave so he could consummate their marriage right then and there.

He was used to being pursued by women. It was a game where he allowed himself to be pounced upon and played with and always walked away when he grew bored.

This situation with Luli was entirely different. He had thought last night, when he had talked her into this marriage, that he had secured the perfect partnership. He could have the sensual wrestling he enjoyed while everything he valued—including detachment from the sort of emotion that weakened lesser mortals—would be protected.

Then he'd tasted a depth of passion unlike anything he'd ever known. It roused a beast that had reacted to the butler's manhandling with atavistic violence.

"Why have you never stood up for yourself with anyone here?" His tone was thick enough with leftover rage she flinched, expression defensive.

"What would I say? Make accusations that would get me thrown out with nothing? He wasn't wrong. I did ingratiate myself with her."

The irony was, her openness about currying favor made her seem vulnerable, provoking the protector in him again. None of this made sense.

He led her down the front steps, still waiting for a miracle where his grandmother came back to life and made clear that he was either correcting her wrong against Luli or told him he was falling for the greatest trick a gold-digger had ever pulled.

"Is that all the luggage, sir?" the chauffeur asked, setting Gabriel's single case in the trunk.

"And that." He nodded at the bag Luli carried. It was the cheap fabric kind the kitchen staff no doubt took to the market stalls for produce.

What had her childhood been like that she thought living like this had been a step *up*? How could such a beautiful, healthy, bright woman be in such a position?

He'd spent half the night reading her code. She hadn't been bluffing about blowing things up, but she'd also layered in failsafes in case she was also locked out. The most critical functions were being monitored electronically so the many people employed by Mae's various enterprises wouldn't be too badly impacted if no one was at the wheel.

Such a perplexing woman.

"What are you doing?" he asked as he realized she was hovering on the bottom step, balking at coming forward to get in the car. The rain had let up, but the humidity was around 1000 percent, making his suit cling to his skin. "Did you forget something?"

"I'm scared." Her clean features were pale in the flat light of overcast skies, her mouth tense, her brow furrowed.

"Of?"

"You. What I've done. Where we're going."

He was having second thoughts himself, but a clench of barbaric implacability insisted he take her away from this place.

"You can't stay here." He wouldn't let her.

"I know." She looked into the car the way someone facing execution might look toward the electric chair.

He scraped together the pieces of himself that still possessed some civility and held out a hand. "It will be all right, Luli."

It wasn't like him to reassure. He enjoyed the feel of a woman's naked body beside him in bed, but he didn't cuddle or coddle. She was causing all sorts of unrecognizable pangs in him, ones that warned him he'd have to proceed carefully where she was concerned, but he still wanted her to come with him.

Now, more than ever.

She tightened her lips with resolve and her grip was clammy. The way she squeezed his fingers filled his chest with inexplicable pressure.

He settled beside her and reminded her to put on her belt.

"Do you think I could get fish someday?" she asked as he turned up the air-conditioning and the car pulled away.

"Odd question, but I don't see why not. I have several aquariums. They're very soothing."

"You do?" She brightened a little. "Will I see them?"

"Of course." It struck him that she would be living with him for the foreseeable future. There was a reason he chose fish as pets. They were quiet and demanded nothing of him.

What the hell had he done?

"Maybe a cat would be better." She set her elbow on the armrest and tucked her fist beneath her chin, speaking to the window now. "Spending your life stuck in a bowl isn't fun."

CHAPTER FIVE

"Is this the right place?" Luli asked with confusion. "Where are the other people?"

"What other people?" Gabriel rose from the car to stand beside her and accepted the umbrella from the chauffeur.

Airports were busy places, weren't they? Gabriel had brought her to a quiet field where stretches of road cut across acres of green toward the blurry horizon. There was an airplane with Arabic writing on its tail parked toward the other end of the low building that crouched behind them. The chauffeur handed their bags to an attendant and they were carried up the stairs in front of them, into an aircraft that was downright intimidating.

It was designed like the ones folded out of paper, with big triangular wings. Like a fighter jet. The windows were a continuous stripe down the body and the tail was painted with the Chinese symbol for dragon. Luli knew that meant it was Gabriel's. He'd been using that symbol in his logos since developing a smartphone game about dragons when he was a boy.

"Don't I have to show a passport to security?"

"It will be waiting for you when we land in Paris."

"Paris!" She swung around. "You said you'd take me to New York." She had tried to teach herself French at one point, but hadn't had anyone to practice with.

"A small detour for shopping." He gave her outfit another disdainful glance and waved to the stairs into the airplane.

Everything was happening so fast. She could barely catch her breath. And now she was awestruck as she entered the jet. It wasn't the kind that looked like a bus with rows of seats and an aisle and little round windows. This was a house. The staff was even lined up exactly as she had stood outside Mae's mansion when he had arrived yesterday.

The pilot welcomed her and invited Gabriel to join him in the cockpit to review their flight path.

"May I show you to your room, Mrs. Dean?" a pretty attendant asked.

"Call me Luli." She needed to talk to Gabriel about how real this marriage was before she ran around calling herself Mrs. Dean. It was still bothering her that he hadn't been nearly as caught up in their kiss as she had been. Then he'd been so angry after the incident with the butler.

With her mind whirling with misgivings, she'd stood on that bottom step as if it had been a jump off a high diving board. She probably wouldn't have come this far if he hadn't held out a hand, reassuring her she could trust him.

Foolishly, she wanted him to keep holding her hand as she followed the woman past the L-shaped sofa and reclining armchairs arranged to face a flat-screen television that hung above a *fireplace*.

Not a house, Luli decided as she absorbed the ebony-and-ivory interior with its glints of chrome and glass. A spaceship.

The attendant took her down a short corridor that ended in a minisuite in grays and chrome. Along with a massive bed, there was a private dining area for two, a sofa, a desk and another television.

"Please use the bell if you need me to bring anything." She pointed at the button near the headboard as she left.

Luli saw her bag hung empty on a hook behind the door. She opened a couple of drawers, finding Gabriel's clothes in them.

Her heart stopped. This was his room.

And there was her underwear in another drawer, looking very paltry in such a big, empty compartment. She closed the cupboard and touched the vase on the night table. It was magnetic, ensuring it wouldn't fall over during turbulence.

She went into the bathroom. Mirrors and subdued lighting turned the powder-blue color scheme silver. The shower had frosted glass and the towels matched the bedspread.

Luli stared at herself in the mirror. Gabriel was right. This double-breasted jacket did her no favors. She had been trying to blend in for so long, she had mostly forgotten how to make the most of her attributes.

There was only soap and lotion in here, no makeup. She washed, then, rather than pin up her hair again, left it loose. The thick, wavy mass had always been one of her best features along with her natural honey-toned skin. She left the jacket on the hook behind the door, even though her plain cotton bra caused unflattering lines against the thin fabric of her knit top.

She paused before she opened the door. Gabriel was on the other side, advising someone on the phone in French what time they would arrive.

She opened the door to see him tossing a pair of bone-colored pants onto the foot of the bed. He noticed her and glanced at the blue shirt on the hanger in his hand. He replaced it on the rack and brought out a red one.

"*Merci*. Au revoir." He ended his call. "These are for you. More comfortable for travel." He pulled the shirt off the hanger and picked up the pants. "And more flattering. Although, that's better without the jacket."

The way his gaze lingered on her made her think of their kiss. Her skin grew tight.

"Thank you," she murmured as she came forward to take the clothes. The linen pants had a wide, woven tape as a drawstring and the shirt was a soft knit with a half dozen buttons at the collar. "We, um, should talk about a few things."

"Sure," he said absently. "I wondered how long it was." His gaze traveled to where tendrils of her hair scrolled against and around the swells of her breast. His hand lifted and she felt a light tug against her scalp, as though he drew a few strands through his finger and thumb, testing its silky texture.

She stood very still, not sure what to make of his curiosity, but liking the tingle that rippled across her scalp and down her nape into her shoulder. It was like their kiss, leaving her feeling shaken, while he had seemed to shake it off.

"I wondered if—" She started to lose her nerve. "We didn't talk about whether this would be, um, a real…um…" She swallowed, voice almost nonexistent as she squeaked, "Marriage?"

His brows came together like a pair of crashing trains, head-on. "You signed the contract. I thought that meant you agreed to everything."

"I didn't have a chance to disagree, did I? Everything happened so fast. Then, the way you kissed me, I thought maybe it was just for show."

"What do you mean? Were *you* pretending when we kissed?" His voice rang with such foreboding, she shivered inwardly.

"N-no?"

"You don't sound sure."

"I'm sure. But I wasn't sure if you…?" She swallowed, completely out of her depth.

"I wasn't pretending anything. I was trying to keep it this side of X-rated."

There was something in his demeanor that reminded her of the time her mother had been photographed with a jaguar. Luli had been seven or eight. Her mother had insisted she join her. Luli had been fascinated by the power and heat radiating off the spotted cat, but the handler had warned her, *Don't look him in the eye.*

So she knew better, but she did it now with this beast—and instantly understood why it was a mistake. It aroused the hunter in him. He might appear relaxed, but his pupils opened and he bared his teeth, sending swirls of reaction into her abdomen. Strangely, it wasn't terror. It was the opposite. An answering type of excitement? She didn't know what it was, but she couldn't look away, couldn't move.

Another tug pulled against her scalp as he turned his finger, winding her hair to draw her forward, until she stood close enough to feel the heat off his body. He let his gaze wander her face, both lazy and thorough, like he was staking a territorial claim.

She found herself studying his mouth, licking her lips.

His fist rested on her shoulder, still tangled in her hair. His thumb stroked along the artery in her throat, where her blood moved thick and unsteady.

"You have the most beautiful skin."

She didn't know how to respond to that and

wasn't given a chance. He dipped his head and opened his mouth against her neck.

This was what they did. They crushed their prey with their powerful jaws.

Except he only breathed hotly against her throat, licked once, sending her pulse skyrocketing. Her breasts prickled and stung inside her bra and a wicked dampness rushed into her loins. She forgot to inhale as he rubbed his lips against her skin. Heat suffused her body and her bones turned to melted wax.

He made a purring noise and scraped his teeth, then sucked lightly, soothing with another lick. The sensation was so enticing, she let her head fall back, fully baring her throat to him.

With another noise of satisfaction, he set a hand on her hip and drew her closer, lifted his head and took her mouth in a kiss that buckled her knees. Hot, thorough, hungry. His arms went around her, pulling her in. Holding her up.

Her arms were tangled in whatever she held, but she didn't care that she couldn't move them. She only wanted more of that raking pleasure of his lips across hers.

The swipe of his tongue against hers sent streaks of electricity through her. She met it with her own, moaning softly in her throat as a near-painful sting heightened every inch of her skin. As if he understood that, he ran his hands over her back and waist and hips, soothing but inciting, making her wriggle restlessly, wanting more.

Her shirt came loose from her waistband and his palms went under the edge, up and up, arriving to cup her breasts so they throbbed with sensitivity in the firm hold of his hands. It was too much and not enough. She could smell something feral on his skin and wanted to drown in that scent. She plucked at his shirt and drew on his tongue and wished she could breathe, but she only wanted *him*.

With a savage hiss of breath, he jerked his head back. The gray-green of his eyes was jungle dark, filled with mysterious shadows and the secrets of life.

Her heart thudded so hard she could feel it rocking her whole body, pulsing in her nipples against his palms and throbbing in the plump folds between her legs.

"Are you faking this?" he asked in a voice that made her scalp prickle.

She looked down at the way his hands were trapped against her breasts under the taut fabric, the clothes he'd given her rumpled on the floor at their feet.

"No." She didn't have a clue what she was doing, but she was lured by the feel of his palms on her breasts to lean in to his touch.

"Good." The word was a satisfied rumble. His thumbs flicked across her nipples, and even muffled by the cotton of her bra, the caress caused a sharp spear of electric sensation to stab into her abdomen. "I'll close the door."

Consciousness began to seep back into her brain. "I was going to save it," she remembered distantly.

"Save what?" His head lowered so the air between their lips became magnetized, tugging with invisible force.

It took all her efforts to remember what they were talking about and say it before he kissed her and erased every thought she could conjure.

"My virginity."

Gabriel stopped a scant millimeter from claiming that luscious, clever mouth. He balanced on the knife's edge between rational thought and the sweetest, blindest escape he could recall glimpsing in his lifetime.

He made his hands slide down to her waist and swallowed.

"You're a virgin?" he asked carefully.

Her tense stomach muscles quivered against the heels of his hands. Her pouted mouth was still parted with invitation. "Yes."

"And you kissed me like that?"

She blinked and the sultry haze of arousal in her sea-green eyes grew tepid and unsure. "Am I not good at it?"

He was hard as high-carbon steel, his flesh nearly searing its way through the layers of cloth between them to get to the molten center of her. He swore he could smell her arousal like nectar, beckoning him to burrow deep. He would give anything to taste her, to feel her arch with pleasure against his mouth.

But he refused to believe what she was suggesting.

"Back up a step."

She took him literally, drawing back so his hands fell to his sides. Her shirt stayed loose, her nipples sharp points against her unbecoming top.

He opened his mouth, closed it. Sought out a couple of brain cells and tried to kick them together, force them to spark cohesive words.

"I'm the first person to ever kiss you? *That's* what you want me to believe?"

"The first *man*." She folded her arms defensively. "There was a boy when I was thirteen. It was…" Her nose wrinkled. "Like pushing my mouth into a pile of mashed potatoes. But there were mostly women in Mae's house so he was my only one."

Gabriel folded. If they were playing poker, she won that hand with a wild-card joker that could be a bluff, but at this point, he could only swear and wave at the clothing on the floor.

"Change. Then go to the lounge. I need a minute to collect myself." Maybe a cold shower. He locked himself in the bathroom the way werewolves chained themselves to a tree on a full moon, so they wouldn't have terrible deeds on their consciences the next day.

He ran his hand down his face as if he could physically bank the heat that had risen in him as he'd contemplated starting their flight in the reclined position.

That had been even better than their first kiss. He hadn't seen any reason to stop except to ensure their privacy, the fines for sitting on the tarmac worth every minute. Hell, they were *married*. If they both wanted it, what was to stop them?

But she was a virgin.

How?

And how hadn't he realized it? He wasn't

a womanizer, but he'd slept with enough women he should be able to recognize a lack of experience in a kiss.

He'd been too carried away by her responsiveness both times to register how untutored she was, though. He liked to lead and she had let him. He'd thought it was a sign they were compatible. If he'd noticed any surprise in her, he'd put it down to his same delight at the way their chemistry ignited so quickly, feeding into each other's arousal in a way that was exponential.

Potentially mind-blowing.

And how was her virginity such a turn-on? He was a normal man with normal fetishes like pretty underwear and high heels. Virginity had never reached the top twenty in his fantasy playlist, but the idea of being Luli's first drew him taut as a piano string.

He skimmed his hand over his hair, tamping down the prickle in his scalp.

The more evidence he collected, the more he was coming to see Luli as every bizarre thing she claimed to be. But the only way to prove she was a virgin was to sleep with her.

And if she was a virgin, he shouldn't touch her.

That paradox wasn't going to torture him at all.

* * *

Luli fought her way out of the clothes she wore, half terrified Gabriel would walk out and see her naked. And reject her again.

Part of her knew he had saved her from being careless and impulsive, but she still felt rebuffed. Like she'd done something wrong. Not morally, although maybe he *was* judging her. She didn't know. But more than that, she feared she had repelled him in some way, out of ignorance.

The drawstring pants hung low on her hips even after she tied them, but they only needed to be turned up twice at the cuff because she was only a little shorter than Gabriel. The shirt seams dropped off her shoulders and the sleeves also needed turning up, but the light knit was soft and comfortable and smelled of him which was disturbing and nice at the same time.

She went to the lounge, sat in one of the armchairs and buckled, then studied the panel in the armrest. Along with several reclining adjustments, there were a dozen massaging options and both heating and cooling settings. She could also control the television, the music, the lights and call the attendant. There were screens of safety instructions and a message from the pilot welcoming them aboard. It showed a countdown to takeoff.

Apparently, they would begin taxiing in seventy-eight seconds.

Gabriel appeared, hair damp as though he'd showered. He removed the shopping bag with twine handles from the other armchair, setting it at her feet before he sat.

"Something for you to play with while we travel."

"Is this your chair? That's why the panel has so many options. I'm sorry." She reached to unbuckle.

"They're exactly the same." He waved her to stay put.

The attendant appeared with a glass on a silver tray that she offered to Gabriel.

"May I bring champagne? Lavender-infused lemonade? Perhaps a cappuccino?"

"Water is fine," Luli said, pressing into her chair.

"Sparkling or Arctic glacier?"

Luli looked to Gabriel, expecting him to make it clear she didn't deserve this level of catering.

"The Canadian spring water for now. No seafood for Luli."

"Thank you, sir. We received that instruction and have arranged alternatives for Mrs.

Dean. The pilot is ready to taxi to the runway if you are?"

"Thank you." He didn't correct her on Luli's title.

The attendant disappeared and the view beyond the windows began to move.

Luli didn't know how to bring up what had happened in his room.

Her downcast gaze landed on the bag, which she had to admit made her curious. It looked like it held black boxes marked with Gabriel's golden dragon logo, all still sealed with cellophane along with something in periwinkle blue.

"Go ahead," he coaxed, sipping as he watched her.

She drew out wireless, noise-canceling headphones, wireless earbuds and other accessories she had only ever seen, mostly online, never dreaming she would use them.

"A new laptop?" And a tablet.

"You'll like it. More processing power. Better security. Consider it a thank-you for making me aware of a vulnerability in my own security program. I've discovered how you broke in and locked me out. Innovative, but it won't happen again."

Luli returned all the boxes to the bag, but kept the periwinkle clutch. It was the most buttery suede she'd ever touched. It had a tiny belt with a gold buckle. A wallet over a smartphone, if she wasn't mistaken. Her ancient flip phone had died years ago and she had only ever held Mae's long enough to fix settings, never needing one of her own because she had no one to call.

The attendant reappeared with her water. "I'll be taking my seat for takeoff. May I set your bag in here?"

She touched a button on the box table next to Luli's chair. The top popped up a few centimeters and slid back to reveal a padded storage bin beneath.

"Thank you," Luli murmured, keeping the wallet in her lap.

"Please don't be alarmed if you hear a noise in the rear of the plane as we ascend. Our design reduces the sonic boom to the decibel of a car door slamming, but you may still notice it. It's perfectly normal." The attendant closed the bin and walked away.

"Your plane travels faster than sound?"

"This one does, yes. There are laws as to where they can be used so I have others for airspaces where we have to travel subsonic."

Others. Plural.

The passage of landscape beyond the windows became a rushing blur before it fell away without any bumps or noises to indicate they had left the ground. She listened and thought she heard the clap, but wasn't sure.

Luli fingered the buckle on the adorable wallet, releasing it to reveal it did conceal a phone. A very feminine and pretty phone in rose-gold-colored metal with crystals embedded around a casing designed with a graceful swoop that set it a world apart from every boring rectangle out there. She wanted to draw it from its custom pocket, to examine it from every angle, but was afraid to mar its shine with her fingerprints.

A light blinked once and a modulated, feminine voice said, "Hello, Luli." The words appeared on the screen then faded against the home screen that showed Gabriel's logo and a handful of icons for apps.

"How—?"

"Facial recognition."

"That's why it took so long to take my passport photo yesterday? You were scanning my face?"

"If you don't like it, you can change it in Settings. I don't always want my phone to open when I glance at it so I also require my fingerprint."

"I know you manufacture all of this technology, but it's still very expensive."

"Very," he interjected dryly. "That's real gold and those are genuine diamonds. Kindly take care of it."

"What?" The priceless phone slipped from her fingers and landed in her lap. She scrambled to pick it up again, mortified. "Why would you give me something like this?"

"You're my wife. People will expect you to have the best."

She shook her head, still not clear on what all was expected of his "wife."

She reached for a sip of water, trying to collect herself, and was promptly distracted by the diamond-cut cubes inside her crystal glass. Judging by the weight, they were plated gold if not solid.

Gabriel's drink was poured over similar chilling stones. Each one was engraved with his dragon symbol.

"You're very different from your grandmother. Mae didn't like her wealth to be obvious. She was afraid people would be encouraged to steal from her if they knew how much she really had."

"Which explains why she kept you locked away and allowed the rest of the staff to think it was okay to treat you poorly. She didn't want anyone to know exactly how much she needed you."

What would it say about her value if he let his staff wait on her and she flaunted the fancy telephone he had given her?

"What was she like?" Gabriel asked. "If my mother told me anything about her, I was too young to remember."

"She didn't care to leave the house. Once she realized how much she could accomplish online, she worked from home and only went into Chen Enterprises for meetings."

"Don't make excuses for her. She didn't take an active role in my life because she didn't approve of her daughter running off to marry an American."

"That's true," she murmured, setting aside her glass. "She had strong views on loyalty and didn't trust easily. Someone must have damaged her trust in the past."

"My mother?" he suggested.

"Perhaps." She closed the pocketbook over the sparkling phone. "But she particularly didn't trust men. It goes back to that business manager, I think. She would only employ a man if he was married and she was introduced to his wife. With her female servants, she didn't want them to be married or have boyfriends, thinking it distracted them and split their loyalty. She fired a maid who was dating without her permission."

"Controlling."

"Yes, but she was kind in her way. I caught a virus once and she had the doctor come, brought me soup and sat with me, even though I was just sleeping." She swallowed back the lump of emotion that swelled in her throat. "I'm going to miss her."

"Have you heard of Stockholm syndrome?" The stones clinked in his glass as he drained it. "It's the bond of trust and loyalty a hostage feels for their captor."

"It wasn't like that." Was it?

Was that what she was starting to feel toward him? She had nearly given him free rein over her body a little while ago, even though she didn't know him well at all.

"She never spoke about my mother other than to complain about her disobedience?" He looked into his empty glass, making it seem a very idle inquiry, but she sensed a deeper need for knowledge inside the question.

"Mae wasn't one to confide or reexamine the past. She never admitted to mistakes or regrets. I only learned she had a daughter when she came back from your father's funeral. I sat in as she directed her attorney to rewrite her will to include you. Until that day, I thought she followed your investments for business reasons."

"Many do."

"I do," she admitted, idly opening a pocket on the wallet to find a metal credit card made of actual platinum. It had an electronic chip on one end, his logo on one side and her name on the other. She shoved it back in its pocket, not ready to contemplate that she had funds at her disposal. "I, um, I've learned a lot from you. I like to imagine that one day I'll have my own money and will manage it wisely and create my own fortune, instead of doing it for someone else."

She smiled at the silly dream of it, but she had needed something to get her through the endless days of feeling like the girl in the tower. A fairy-tale fantasy of building her own castle was a lot more fun to dwell on than facing the reality of her situation or worrying there was a darker future in store for her.

Never in her wildest imaginings had she pictured *this*.

"I think your grandmother was proud of you," she said.

His dark brow went up with skepticism.

"I don't mean that as flattery. Maybe I should say she took a certain amount of credit for your success."

"Her DNA made me what I am? Perhaps.

God knows I didn't get any hidden talents from my father. But I'm beginning to think she owes *her* success to *you*."

"I would never make such a claim." Not without expecting a sharp rebuke from Mae.

The plane leveled off and the ultrapleasant attendant appeared with a fresh drink for Gabriel and a fresh smile for Luli. "May I bring anything to ensure your comfort?"

"The lavender thing is popular. You should try it," Gabriel advised.

She *was* curious. She nodded.

"There's a lovely iced-mint cookie that pairs with it. I'll bring that, too." The attendant melted away.

"You don't have to be so…nice." Luli wondered what the attendant was going to say to the rest of the crew behind her back. "Do you feel sorry for me or something?"

"You told me what you were worth, Luli. Act like you believe it."

Gabriel came to Paris at least once a year and almost always with a woman. He didn't consider his sexual partners as objects to be "kept," but he liked to think of himself as a generous partner in bed and in boutiques. More than one lover had accused him of offering material items in lieu of his thoughts and feelings, which he couldn't refute. He had developed the habit of keeping both of those things firmly to himself.

If asked, he blamed his martial arts training for his circumspection. Deep down, he knew it was simply his nature to be aloof. He had never cultivated close friendships and had always felt a step apart from regular society. Did it stem from a broken heart after losing his mother so young? From fear of turning into the drunken shell his father had become? That was likely part of it, but people who spoke their thoughts aloud or permitted emotion to rule them only got back more of the same. Physical feelings of hunger and sexual desire were distraction enough. He had no wish to *yearn*.

And sometimes, when he was in a particularly introspective mood, he suspected that the wealth he had accumulated was both a strategy against wanting any of those abstract things that seemed to be so important to other people and a buffer against the world at large. He shouldered immense responsibility for people's jobs and the infrastructure that served their lives and influenced whether the stock market went up or down on a given day, but he employed armies of people to look after all of that. He spoke to very few people in any meaningful way. A professional of some kind or another could be hired to do almost anything that he didn't care to do himself so that's what he did.

But he couldn't do that with Luli.

She didn't fit the compartment of employee or lover or any other label he had previously slotted people under—not even estranged blood relative. He'd gone and *married* her, which made him personally responsible for her. People could be hired to feed his fish, but who would feed *her* if he didn't see to it?

Who would tell her, "It's okay. Go."

She stayed put, only her nose poking out the open jet door like a cat testing the air, sapphire eyes taking in the pale pink clouds of the evening sky, the car on the tarmac below and the people waiting beside it.

"There's someone in a uniform down there," she reported and backed into him.

The feel of her was erotic and enticing and caused a strange sensation to flutter through Gabriel. It wasn't unlike the aggression that had gripped him in that moment with the butler. Protectiveness, he realized as his hands went to her upper arms in both an effort to reassure her and a claim of warning to anyone who might threaten her.

"The customs agent." He made himself release her. "It's fine. Go ahead."

She cautiously went down the stairs before him. His assistant met her with a smile and an envelope. "Your passport, Mrs. Dean."

"Really?" She hurried to look inside.

"If I may?" the customs agent asked, taking the passport long enough to glance at the stamp inside it. "*Merci.* Enjoy your stay." He handed it back to her. "Mr. Dean, nice to see you again. *Toutes nos félicitations.*" He tipped his cap and walked away.

"Thank you," Luli said with bewilderment to his retreating back.

"Your birth certificate is in there with your marriage certificate and my contact details," his assistant continued. "Please reach out at any time with questions or concerns. I'm Mr. Dean's feet on the ground here in Europe, but I can quickly direct any inquiries to another party if it's outside my bailiwick."

"Thank you." Luli's eyes were big as beach balls, glossy and bright. She blinked rapidly.

Gabriel nodded his thanks and steered her into the back of the car.

Luli's hands shook as she tried to pull the certificate from the envelope without damaging its pristine condition.

"It is my birth certificate," she said to him with awe. "This is me."

"Good," he commented.

Her hands continued to shake as she took great care folding the document exactly right so it fit into a pocket of her blue wallet. She transferred her passport and his assistant's card and their marriage certificate into the same pocket, then secured the zipper, anchoring the little tab with her thumb.

"Are you cold?" He reached to take hold of her hand, only wanting to test her temperature.

She twisted her hand to squeeze his tightly and turned a wet look on him. "Thank you," she choked, using her free hand to press the wallet into her navel.

"Why are you crying?" Alarmed, he reached for the box of handkerchiefs, each square of ultrasoft bamboo dyed a different shade from ruby to emerald to amethyst.

"Because—" Her voice broke. She dabbed one beneath her eyes, then beneath her nose. "I don't know how I'll pay you back for this, but I will. I promise."

"For what? It was nothing." He had paid a premium to fast-track the paperwork, but the fees were a tenth of what his chauffeur carried in his money clip for incidentals.

"No, *I* was nothing. Now I have the most important thing in the world. *Me*." She wrapped both hands around the wallet and pressed it between her breasts, breathing still shaky. "Thank you."

You told me what you were worth, Luli. Act like you believe it.

She *had* been acting. The whole time. Still was, especially as a handful of designers whose names she knew from Mae's glossy magazines behaved with deference as they welcomed her to a private showroom complete with catwalk.

She had to fight back laughing with incredulity as they offered her champagne, caviar, even a pedicure.

"I—" She glanced at Gabriel, expecting him to tell them she aspired to model and should be treated like a clothes horse, not royalty.

"A full wardrobe," he said. "Top to bottom, morning to night, office to evening. Do what you can overnight, send the rest to my address in New York."

"*Mais bien sûr, monsieur,*" the couturier said without a hint of falter in her smile. "Our pleasure."

"Gabriel—" Luli started to protest as the women scattered.

"You remember what I said about this?" he tapped the wallet that held her phone. "I need you to stay on-brand."

"Reflect who you are?"

"Yes."

"Who are you?" she asked ruefully. "I only met you ten minutes ago."

"I'm a man who doesn't settle for anything less than the best." He touched her chin. "The world is going to have a lot of questions about why we married. Give them an answer."

His words roused the competitor who still lurked inside her. She wanted to prove to the world she was *worthy* to be his wife. Maybe she wanted to prove her worth to him, too. Definitely she longed to prove something to herself.

Either way, she made sure those long-ago years of preparation paid off. She had always been ruthless in evaluating her own shortcomings and knew how to play to her strengths. She might not be trying to win a crown today, but she hadn't been then, either. She'd been trying to win the approval of a woman who hadn't deserved her idolatry.

She pushed aside those dark memories and clung instead to the education she had gained in those difficult years.

"That neckline will make my shoulders

look narrow," she said, making quick up-down choices. "The sweetheart style is better, but no ruffles at my hips. Don't show me yellow. Tangerine is better. A more verdant green. That one is too pale." In her head, she was sectioning out the building blocks of a cohesive stage presence. Youthful, but not too trendy. Sensual, but not overtly sexual. Charismatic without being showy.

"Something tells me I'm not needed," Gabriel said twenty minutes in and rose to leave. "We'll go for dinner in three hours." He glanced to the couturier. "And return in the morning for another fitting."

"*Parfait. Merci, monsieur.*" Her smile was calm, but the way people were bustling told Luli how big a deal this was. How big a deal *Gabriel* was.

The women took her measurements while showing her unfinished pieces that only needed hemming or minimal tailoring so she could take them immediately.

"You'll be up all night," Luli murmured to one of the seamstresses.

The young woman moved quickly, but not fast enough for her boss who kept crying, *"Vite! Vite!"*

"I'm sorry to put you through this," Luli added.

"*Pas de problème*. Monsieur Dean is a treasured client. It's our honor to provide your trousseau." She clamped her teeth on a pin between words. "Do you know where he's taking you for dinner? We should choose that dress next, so I can work on the alterations while you have your hair and makeup done. It must be fabulous. The world will be watching."

She would be presented publicly as his wife, Luli realized with a hard thump in her heart.

She still didn't know what their marriage meant. He had remained silent on the topic of their sleeping together after her confession before they left Singapore. They had spent the flight talking about the features of his laptop and some investments she thought she should unload, since their value had peaked and would likely begin to dwindle as the news of his takeover sank in. He had approved it, allowing her to continue ensuring the cogs of Mae's business kept turning while he chewed his way through the wiring into her accounts himself.

They had dozed in their recliners at different times, neither of them seeking the comfort of the bed. He hadn't invited her to join him there, at least. She hadn't known how to circle back to whether he wanted her there.

She wished she knew what he was thinking, now that she had confessed her virginity. She wished she had experience to draw on! Had he kissed her because he found her attractive? Or merely because she had signed a paper that allowed him conjugal rights? She met all the criteria for typical standards of modern beauty, but perhaps that only made her objectively attractive and didn't translate into someone who was actually desirable.

She reminded herself again that he had done her a favor in cutting things short. Along with youth and beauty, one of the few things she possessed that was hers to give or barter was her virginity. She had presumed it might have value to certain men, but Gabriel didn't seem to be one of them.

And yet he must like sex and women. She stood where other women must have stood, buying clothing charged to him. Gabriel was a *treasured client*.

How strange to hate women she had never met, but she did. Instantly and bitterly.

Jealousy is a sign of insecurity and low self-esteem, she could hear her mother cautioning her. But this wasn't a case where Luli could size up her competition and see how many of their qualities she possessed then make adjustments to outshine them.

She could only make the most of what she had—and gritted her teeth in determination, intending to.

"This one," she said of the dress she tried on a few minutes later.

From the back, it was a one-shouldered evening dress in cranberry silk with a filmy chiffon skirt, except half of the skirt was ivory. The front was more dramatic, with its silk bodice fitted to her breasts and the bottom of the dress made of shiny silk and cut to miniskirt height. The chiffon of the overskirt was belted in the pink-red silk, but its ruffled edges opened as she walked, delicate as fairy wings.

"You have a good eye and the ideal figure for Madame's creations," her seamstress gushed.

Luli accepted tall silver shoes with a pop of merlot on the sole then moved to the styling room. Her hair was blown out and her nails buffed and polished. A cosmetician applied cleansers, toners, moisturizer, antioxidants and foundation. When the woman reached for her color palette, Luli said, "I'll do it."

It had been years, but her muscle memory for liquid eyeliner and blending hues to contour her bone structure served her well.

Even so, when she stood dressed and ready

in front of the mirror, she saw a stranger. Not because it had been so long since she had seen herself stage ready, but because she was no longer fourteen. Being twenty-two shouldn't have made such a difference when she had been acting like an adult as an adolescent, but it did. Rather than looking like a girl playing dress up, she looked like a woman. A confident, self-possessed, beautiful woman.

Act like you believe it, she silently told the apprehensive face in the mirror.

"Monsieur Dean has arrived," her seamstress came in to advise her. "*Ooh, là là!* He will faint. I may." She fanned her face.

"Thank you," Luli said, accepting the compliment graciously, as her mother had taught her to do. Anything less would suggest she believed herself inferior in some way.

Luli gave herself a final scrutiny, adjusted her posture and ensured she stood as tall as she was able. Then she thought back to the puppy she had played with as a child. She didn't recall whom it had belonged to, but the memory was one she had always used to awaken a feeling of happiness within her. It was the happiest she'd ever felt.

She faltered. Had she really not had a happy moment since then?

"Perhaps you would like to carry this

instead?" the seamstress said, offering a
Cleopatra clutch in black alligator skin with
an ornate silver clasp.

Luli had kept her wallet in her line of sight
the entire time she'd been here, terrified that
if it disappeared, *she* would. She used the excuse of changing purses to check *again* that
her precious identification was still in her
possession. She handed off the empty wallet
to the woman who promised to bag it with
the items going to the car.

Emotion threatened to swamp her afresh
as she absorbed what Gabriel had given her
with a few legal documents. Options. Possibility. The gift of existence was greater than
any haute couture dress or designer handbag
or limitless credit card.

It was a miracle.

She *did* have a more recent memory of happiness, she realized. This. As she snapped
the clutch closed and turned its tiny lock,
she let the glow of gratitude toward him seep
through her until joy shone from her smile
and radiated from her demeanor.

With every ounce of grace she had ever
possessed, she walked to the reception lounge.

Gabriel turned from instructing the couturier
to box up as much as possible by morning so

they could take it on the jet with them—and all the air was punched from his lungs.

A goddess approached in an unhurried gait that rocked her hips. Her skirt wafted back from her mile-long legs and her breasts bounced lightly above a long, slender waist. Her hair slithered in loose ribbons of caramel with glints of cool platinum against the warm gold of her bare shoulders and upper chest.

Her face was an angel's, luminous and pure. Aside from the dramatic lines that accented her eyes and gave them a hint of tilt, she wore little makeup. Or wore it so well, it was barely noticeable. Her lashes were naturally long and thick. He'd studied them while she had slept on the plane. Her succulent lips were accentuated with a delicate pink and shone with gloss. Her smile was one of exultation. Whatever she was celebrating, he decided she was entitled to it.

He couldn't fault her in that moment for one damned thing.

She halted before she reached him, struck a pose, pivoted to show the back of the dress. It lifted and floated back down before she pivoted again and continued toward him with a playful sparkle in her eye.

The entire move had been executed so smoothly, he chuckled with enjoyment.

"Maximum points for first impression, I hope. Otherwise we start again." She met his gaze without shyness, smiling, utterly composed.

She was sexy as hell.

Virgin, he reminded himself, yet the only thing that kept him from ravishing her on the spot was their rapt audience.

She was waiting for his judgment, he realized, as she continued looking at him and he noted tension creep in around her smile. The flutter of her pulse in her throat grew more rapid, exactly as it had been when she had quietly challenged him in his grandmother's office.

"You broke the scale." He brought her hand to his mouth, wanting to place his lips in far more intimate places than her soft knuckle. "And good thing because I'm too hungry to wait while you start again. This is for you."

He gently splayed out her hand and threaded the ring onto her finger.

It was a performance for their audience and she gasped with appropriate amazement at the fifteen-carat marquise-cut blue diamond. Its split shank was coated in white diamonds to set off the rare color of the center stone.

The women around them squealed with excitement.

"I don't know what to say," Luli said faintly.

"Thank you?" he suggested dryly, and did what was expected, taking her into his arms for a kiss.

Her arms went around his neck and her heart pounded so hard he felt it against his chest, teasing his own to come race with hers. He kept the kiss light, not wanting to ruin her lipstick, but her lips clung shyly to his and she slid her lashes down with awareness as he released her.

He groaned inwardly. Virgin she might be, but her response to his touch was the most erotic thing he'd ever experienced.

"Good night, ladies. Your extra effort won't go unrewarded," he said with a nod.

Voices wished them a lovely evening and he escorted her to the car, for once anticipating the entrance they would make. Women invariably wanted to be seen with him, whether it was an innocent business meeting or a lengthy, more intimate association. He found the quest for attention tiresome, but accepted it.

With Luli, however, he was already smiling inwardly at the stir she would cause. He usually only felt this sense of excitement when one of his personal projects went to market— a niche app or something else he had poured himself into developing.

He was swelling with pride, he realized, but not of ownership. He didn't take credit for this transformation or even for the discovery of her.

No, he was simply proud to be with a woman who shone brighter than the midday sun.

CHAPTER SIX

THE RESTAURANT WAS a converted house in the Sixth Arrondissement, once owned by an art dealer. It brimmed with impressionist paintings and priceless objets d'art. A murmur went through the diners in the main lounge and piano bar as they were shown through to an atrium with only one table that was obviously reserved for the most illustrious customers.

A small fountain and an abundance of ferns provided a modicum of privacy, but the glass walls and ceiling provided none. Luli didn't care who looked at them. She was too busy taking in the fat moon above the glittering Eiffel Tower.

"I've wanted to come to Paris since I first understood what it was. I can't believe I'm here," Luli said, trying not to betray her complete awe.

"We'll come back soon. I have to get back

to some meetings I left when you texted about my grandmother."

"Was that a flash?" She looked toward the fountain.

"Outside? Yes."

"No, from—"

A jewel-bedecked customer had crept to the fountain and held a smartphone in the air space behind the streaming water, aiming it at them. One of the servers in a black vest and long white apron hurried to draw the woman away.

"Ignore it," Gabriel said. "My security team will address it."

She couldn't. Glints of light were popping against the wall of shrubbery beyond the atrium's walls and on the rooftop of the adjacent building.

"I used to dream of being so famous everyone would want my photo. It's quite intrusive, isn't it? How do you stand it?"

"Honestly, I'm not of much interest to the paparazzi unless I'm with a woman. Even then, it very much depends on who she is. I met with a married actress a couple of times, years ago. She was researching a part. It was completely innocuous, but she was of a mind that any publicity was good publicity. She tipped off photographers every time and the entertainment sites made it into something it wasn't. The movie did well at the box office and on the award circuit. Perhaps her strategy had some weight." He told her whom it had been. She was quite famous, but old enough to be his mother.

Their wine was delivered and poured. Luli didn't know where to look. Outside at the cameras? At the craning necks in the main part of the restaurant? Looking at Gabriel would only get her tangled up in his gaze.

"I suppose your connection to your grandmother makes you news right now," she murmured, studying the ornate silver stem and the patterns etched into the tulip-shaped red bowl of her one-of-a-kind handcrafted wineglass—or so their server had informed her.

"My grandmother's connection to me affects people who have business dealings with Chen Enterprises. I'm already so rich. No one could care less that I just got richer."

"But you said the paparazzi only pay attention to you if the woman you're with is famous. They don't know who I am."

"Exactly." One corner of his mouth went up in a cynical curl. "The waitstaff is going to make a bundle in tips from people wanting your name. Joke's on them. I didn't offer it."

"They wouldn't recognize it anyway. I'm nobody."

The waiter brought an amuse-bouche—a spoon that held a deviled quail's egg on a mushroom cap with a glazed baby carrot next to it.

"It seems silly that anyone would care," she continued. "I'm as guilty as the next person for following celebrity gossip. Your grandmother subscribed to overseas magazines and I love royal wedding photos and the like, but—*oh*."

"You've arrived. Welcome." His lingering smile held gentle mockery. "Yes, everyone is trying to be the first to report on my marriage. More pointedly, to *whom*."

"I suppose that is news." *She* was. She sobered as she recalled how attentive the *couturier* and her staff had been. "Was there someone else they expected? Are you *with* someone?" She should have asked that several kisses ago.

"Only you," he said dryly. "A press release goes out at midnight explaining I've been quietly courting my grandmother's business manager and we've made it official."

"No one is going to believe that. Or that I'm a business manager." She thought of the butler trying to throw her out on her ear, first chance he got.

"It doesn't matter what they believe, only what I know. While you were playing dress up, I accessed the backup files and ran some reports for my edification. You make a lot of small adjustments that make a big difference. You do, in fact, manage her business affairs."

"Mae liked me to be vigilant."

"But you did much of it electronically. I saw the scripts you inserted to alert you when something falls outside your parameter sets. You've been playing with my back end for a while."

She had, but he didn't need to make it sound so suggestive.

Their plates were exchanged. A light shell of something that might have been egg white had been quick fried into a lacy web and bent into a basket while warm. It held a leg of squab, a half dozen bright green peas and a dollop of what she learned was whipped turnip. A smear of chili sauce framed it and violets were sprinkled for decoration.

"If you've gone that far," she said, hand going to the clutch in her lap. "You're able to restore from backup and lock me out."

"I could. But I refuse to take the easy way. I won't let you get the better of me."

"Because I'm a woman?"

"I'm competitive, not sexist."

"How did *you* learn to code?" She snapped a strand from the basket and discovered it was made of sharp cheese, rich and salty against her tongue.

"My grade school had three afterschool clubs—computers, arts and athletics. I didn't want to go home, so I had to pick one. I can speak on a stage if I have to, but I have no talent for performing or other creative pursuits. I was decent in track and field, but have no interest in team sports. The isolation of a computer screen, however, was my dream habitat."

"Why didn't you want to go home?"

"My father was a drunk and not fun to be around."

"I'm sorry."

"It's not your fault."

She couldn't help noticing the strain of his shirt across his chest, as though his muscles had tensed despite the fact he sounded very indifferent and relaxed.

"I read that you're a black belt in kung fu."

"It's a good workout and clears my mind."

"When did you start?"

"When bullies started calling me Kung Fu Kid." He pointed at the tiny overlap at the corner of his eye. "I went to the nearest dojo and offered my computer skills in exchange for lessons. It was another convenient way to avoid going home."

"Did you teach those bullies a lesson?"

"My *sifu* taught me not to care what they said."

"You never fought back?" What was the point in going all the way to black belt, then?

"I threw a boy to the ground once, when he tried to start something. His friends were right there, planning to help. Word got around and they stopped bothering me. Then I sold my app and everyone wanted to be my friend."

"You were twelve? It was a game, wasn't it?"

"This is why I never bother talking about myself. Anything of note has already been documented online." He cleaned the meat off the delicate bone in one bite and set it aside.

"I don't know much more than that, except that you won a national competition for young entrepreneurs and caught the attention of Silicon Valley. They paid you a million dollars?"

"Which caught my grandmother's attention. She came to warn me not to let my father take control of my money. He cautioned me against trusting her. They had a heated discussion and I didn't hear from her again until she came to his funeral."

"She didn't try to help you? Did she realize your father had a drinking problem?"

"Given how furious she was with my mother, I believe she probably did. I didn't want her help."

"Why not?"

"My own version of Stockholm syndrome, I suppose. The devil you know and all that."

She absorbed that, thinking he was onto something. She had rationalized staying with Mae rather than taking the hard road of striking out on her own. Before that, she had tried relentlessly and earnestly to earn her mother's regard.

"Did you keep control of your money?" she asked.

"More or less. I hired a certified advisor and talked my father into paying off our mortgage, which had been my grandmother's advice."

"Real estate has been very good to her."

"And me. I invested heavily in property as I sold more apps. It came easily to me. Felt like a license to print money. When I was fifteen, I hired a private tutor so I had more flexibility with my education. I graduated high school early and completed a business degree before I turned twenty. I predicted the financial crash and was one of those select few who came up roses."

"And your father…?"

"Drank himself to kidney failure, but lived comfortably until then. I supported him, put him in rehab several times. It never took." He used a jagged corner of shell to stab a pea and ate it with a crunch.

"Did he have other family? Do you have cousins?"

"A handful of people who didn't want to know him, but who crawl out of the woodwork periodically to ask me for start-up capital. Some ventures succeed, others have gone bust. It's another reason I've kept my distance from my grandmother. It's hard to say no to family, but it can be foolish to say yes. Do you have family besides your mother and father? Is he still alive?"

"I haven't seen anything online about him since he went to prison for corruption a couple of years after I left for Singapore. I guess his sons are my half brothers, but I've never met them or tried to reach out." She wrinkled her nose in dismay. "I presume they're much like him. My mother's family was very poor. She never spoke of them. I wouldn't know where to begin looking for them and have no reason to."

It was odd to talk about herself. No one had asked about her life or seemed interested in it for years.

Their plates were cleared and bowls of warm, scented water brought to rinse their hands.

"We should dance," Gabriel said when she looked toward the drift of piano notes from the other side of the restaurant.

She shook her head. "I took ballet years ago, but only to help with grace and posture. I've never danced for real."

"With a man, you mean? That's a good reason to do it, then, isn't it?" He rose and held out his hand. "Leave that here," he said of the clutch she would have carried with her. "It's perfectly safe."

She nervously left it on the chair as she rose and placed her hand in his. An electric current seemed to run from the weave of their fingers up her arm to start an engine purring in her chest.

Eyes followed them, but she kept her gaze on the lobe of Gabriel's ear as he wound through the tables ahead of her. Out of nowhere, she wondered what it would be like to nibble his ear. People did that, didn't they? Would he like it? Tendrils of intrigue unfurled inside her at the thought of dabbling her tongue there and sucking. Of him doing it to her. She had to stifle a reflexive moan at the carnal fantasy.

Along with the pianist, there were a cellist and a violinist. It was like being in a movie as he turned when they reached the dance floor and drew her into his arms. She felt as though she floated when they began to move together.

"You're perfect," he said as he led with athletic grace.

Her light skirt lifted and fell against her bare legs in a sensual caress while she absorbed the strength of him, the surety of his touch moving her about so effortlessly. A pleasurable heat suffused her and she knew this would be her new memory for her stage smile. She didn't know if she'd ever felt so light in her life. So carefree and purely, simply *happy*.

She suspected she was actually asleep and would wake in her plain room in the servants' quarters of Mae's mansion very soon.

"The entire place is spellbound," he murmured, making her falter slightly.

"Was that the goal?"

"I can't deny I wanted to see their reaction."

"Why?" She became self-conscious and had to concentrate to ensure she didn't misstep.

"A crowd like this is used to being surrounded by beauty. You're above and beyond anything they will have ever seen."

"Is that what I am? A piece of art you've acquired?" Was that why he hadn't said anything about their kiss?

His mouth was no longer relaxed. "No."

"What, then? A project? A percentage?"

"I have no idea. You're unlike anything *I've* ever encountered."

"But you want to twirl me around and say, *Look what I found.*"

"I want to feel you in my arms." His voice was low and powerful enough to resonate through her.

Somehow he kept them moving without bumping into anyone while she tried to read his eyes. She didn't know what she was seeing in those rocky ocean depths.

"You haven't said anything since I told you," she reminded him.

"Is it true?" he demanded.

"I'm looking to you for guidance because I have no idea what I'm doing." She spoke with a thread of wildness in her voice. The sense of spinning beyond herself was growing as she realized exactly how much she was looking to him—because she was that far out of her depth in every single way.

His cheek ticked. "I wish I knew whether I could believe you."

"What reason would I have to lie?"

"The twenty million I just dropped on clothes and shoes, perhaps?"

"You didn't." She stopped dancing. The world continued to sway and swirl. She thought she might faint as all her lifeblood dropped into her feet. "Please say it wasn't that much."

"With the ring, closer to thirty. It's Paris, Luli. What did you think?"

Sequin-covered bikinis and formal evening gowns were expensive, but they were the price of pageant entry, maybe the cost of bus fare or a flight to get to the competition. They weren't the value of a district's worth of housing. What had she done? She clung to his sleeve to keep herself upright, vision hazy as she absorbed that she had indebted herself to him far beyond anything she could have imagined.

His arms firmed around her, supporting her. "Look at me. Are you all right?"

"I think I'm going to be sick."

If he had wanted to create a sensation, mission accomplished. Speculation about his mysterious new wife would shift to whether she was carrying his child as she paled and leaned into him.

"Come sit down." He led her back to their table.

She took her clutch into her lap and, he suspected, checked for her passport, judging by the furtive movement beneath the edge of the table.

"Have a sip of water," he ordered. "Then tell me why you're upset." She had handled the shopping like a pro. He wasn't complaining about the cost, only pointing out that it made for a strong motive where manipulating his emotions was concerned.

"Why would you do that?" Her hand shook as she sipped. Tears brimmed her mink lashes. "I'll never be able to pay you back. *Never.*"

"I don't expect you to."

The waiter brought their next course and she turned her face to the window to hide her distress. Gabriel waved him off from pouring fresh wine.

The single braised lamb chop with watercress and candied pistachios was decorated with a sprig of rosemary, pearl onions and dots of orange and mint sauces. Gabriel thought it looked appetizing, but Luli looked at her plate with misery. He didn't dare tell her that the lamb had been flown in fresh from New Zealand this morning and the six vintage wine pairings they would sample with each course were thousands of euros each.

Minutes ago, she'd been incandescent, fully enjoying herself. Her mood had started to dim when she had asked if she was a project for him.

"Luli." He set his hand palm-up on the table, wanting her to look at him. "I told you I don't pay for sex. I don't buy women. You don't owe me anything."

"I keep thinking I'll wake up in my room. I wish I would." She pinched her arm.

That bare cell of a room with not so much as a family photo or a glimmer of vibrant beauty that was *her*? *No.*

"I shouldn't have started this," she said with a despairing shake of her head. "I wanted to take control. I thought I could handle it, even if it was difficult. It was very hard when I arrived in Singapore, but I got through it. I'm a strong person," she insisted, but sounded like she was trying to convince herself. "This is too much."

Her gaze finally met his and the rawness she exposed clawed at his heart.

"Whatever you think you can turn me into, I'm *not*." She looked to the windows, then the other direction, then the ceiling, as though she sought escape and realized she was cornered. Her breasts rose against the binding of her dress, plumping with each shaking breath.

"Luli." He wiggled his fingers. "Give me your hand. This is culture shock. That's all."

"Culture shock!" She blinked and a tear fell to glisten diamond sharp on her cheekbone. Her hands stayed in her lap.

"Culture assault," he corrected dryly. He should have anticipated it. Even his top executives dropped their jaws and bumbled with nerves when they caught a glimpse of how he lived. "Would you like to leave?"

"Does it matter what I want? Why did I think I should fight so hard or reach so high? It's not as though I could make myself matter by wearing new clothes and going outside. I'm still *nothing.*"

"We're going all the way to existential crisis? Come on, then. We'll take this somewhere more private." As he helped her into the car moments later, she heard him tell his driver, "Cancel the helicopter. We'll go to the apartment."

"Where were you going to take me in a helicopter?" she asked twenty minutes later, when he joined her on the balcony of his modern penthouse.

The colorful reflections on the Seine were smudged lines through the sparkling cityscape below. The Eiffel Tower was so big before her, she could have reached out and touched it.

She was still overwhelmed, still feeling like she was on stage, wearing this gown, but the bricked patio was about the size of Mae's courtyard. The darkness turned down the volume on how alien the world had become, giving her a chance to catch her breath and grapple her emotions back under control.

"I was going to take you to my *château*. Do you want anything? I could order take-out noodles and roast pork. That might feel more familiar."

"You have a house *and* a flat here?"

"I've been restoring the *château* since I bought it two years ago. I've never stayed there. It was built in the sixteen hundreds as a folly for the King's mistress and has become one of mine. I have to park my money somewhere." He leaned his elbows on the wall and studied the city below them.

At the word *mistress*, she had to ask. "Why did you want to take me there?" For seduction?

"It's pretty. I thought you'd like it. At least I thought that a few hours ago, when I made the arrangements and you were having fun spending my money."

"Why did you *let* me? I don't understand what you want from me," she said with a throb in her voice. "Am I a white elephant, more curse than blessing? A pretty adornment for your arm? Am I supposed to sleep with you because you saved me? Because we're *married*?"

"One way or another, you were going to save yourself. We both know that, Luli." His voice was firm and strong, if a shade rueful. "All I'm doing is adding accelerant."

"Why?"

"Because you're a riddle. I enjoy puzzles."

"I want to be a woman. My own woman," she said, soft and fierce.

But she was realizing that leaving Mae's house and building a new, independent life were two very different things. There was a wide chasm that had to be bridged and she didn't have the skills or resources to do it.

He sighed. "If I see you as a woman, I'll want to sleep with you."

She hugged herself and rubbed her arms, even though she wasn't cold. In fact, she grew warm. Empty in a way that longed for him to hold her and kiss her and fill her with all those sensations that made the world a magical place.

"What's so bad about that?"

"You said you were saving your virginity," he reminded. "For who?"

"I don't know. You? You're supposed to wait, aren't you? For your wedding night?"

A long, tense silence.

"I haven't," he finally stated.

She sighed, admitting heavily, "I thought it might mean something to whoever it was. Have value. Maybe even if I was desperate—"

"Your virginity is not a commodity, Luli," he cut in sharply. "Your body isn't. Save yourself for a relationship that matters. Someone special."

"So you don't…" She swallowed. "Want me? Because I'm a virgin?"

"Have you looked in a mirror? Of course I want you. I'm saying don't have sex with the first man you marry."

She choked on a laugh, recognizing it as a joke, but *they were married.*

"You talked about becoming a trophy wife and that led me to believe you were experienced. Given that you're not…" His voice became tight with reluctant honor. "I don't know that we should go there. You would want what every woman eventually asks for and I can't give you that."

"Children? I don't want them. Not for a long

time, if ever. That's totally fine if you can't make them."

Another pointed silence, then a husk of a laugh.

"I was going to say love, but you continue to confound me." He straightened and leaned his hip against the low wall. "Why don't you want children?"

"I can't even take care of myself!" She waved a helpless hand through the air.

"You're so blind." He reached out and gave a tendril of her hair a small tug. "My grandmother employed two hundred people directly, not to mention the ten or so thousand who work for companies in which she invests. Who looks after all of them? Her? No."

"That was with *her* money and resources. I don't even have pajamas. I'll be sleeping in the clothes you gave me on the airplane." She wondered where they were.

Wondered why he couldn't love her. Far above Paris and freedom and all the other fantasies she had ever had was the dream that one day she would be loved. Was she not worthy of such a thing? Why not?

"Silly girl," he said. "You have six cases of ready-to-wear in the guest room. Didn't you hear the bell when the concierge delivered them?"

"What bell? *Six?* Gabriel, I can't!"

"Don't start hyperventilating again. Come on. I want to show you something. You'll like it." He took her hand in his warm one and drew her inside.

Her heels clicked on the herringbone pattern in the parquet floor of the hall. The penthouse was bigger than the bottom floor of Mae's sprawling mansion, but this was located atop a skyscraper. It was modern, but filled with old-world touches in the wainscoting and crown moldings. A castle in the sky.

"Your room," he said, pushing open a door into a darkened room where a half dozen suitcases stood at the foot of a wide bed. "But come into mine."

Her heart rate picked up.

He didn't turn on any lights as they entered the massive room with the massive bed. She barely looked that direction or took in anything else. She was drawn to the primordial glow of the floor-to-ceiling aquarium.

She gasped, pulled forward by the muted burble to feast her eyes on the iridescent blues and neon pinks, the fierce reds and flashing yellows. Spots adorned long lacy tails that swished in slow motion while striped orange missiles darted into crevices in the colorful fingers of coral and swaying blades of sea grass.

She didn't know where to look and grew dizzy trying to take it all in. She wanted to lean against the glass, breath fogging upon it as she watched.

"You like?" His arm came around her waist and she leaned into him, overwhelmed, but this time in a way that was gentle and full of wonder.

"Your grandmother's pond only had koi. They were pretty, but nothing like this. It's so beautiful."

"Can you see the tub on the other side?" he pointed. "I'll run you a bath and you can watch the fish, then dream all night that you're swimming with them."

She wanted to laugh, but his arm around her felt so nice her own arms reached to encircle him on instinct, needing to cling to him for fear of going adrift.

"No one has hugged me since—" She couldn't remember. A long, long time ago. She welled up and began to shake.

"Shh." His hand offered a soothing caress against her ribs. "Keep it together, Luli. I'm useless with tears."

He wasn't, though. As she began to sob in earnest, he shifted so she was pressed fully to his front. He held her in a firm embrace that kept her from breaking into a thousand disjointed pieces and spoke against the part in her hair.

"It's okay. You're not in there. You're out here. *Breathe*."

CHAPTER SEVEN

DESPITE A LONG BATH after her breakdown, Luli didn't dream of the fish. She dreamed of Gabriel's arms around her and his soothing voice and his strong hand rubbing her back. She dreamed he was beside her in the bed, his hands on her breasts and seeking their way into other secretive places.

But he wasn't. And she woke in a sweat, loins aching, embarrassed with herself for such erotic fantasies.

The lingering memory made her self-conscious as she emerged from her room, dreading making eye contact, but Gabriel was on the phone behind the closed door of his office—which perversely made her disappointed.

A servant invited her to a table in a nook that caught the morning sun and overlooked the Seine. She brought her a blessedly familiar breakfast of rice porridge and *kaya* toast with soft eggs. Afterward, Luli took her second cup of French-press coffee to the balcony where she listened to the city noises that were both the same and different from the ones she had heard beyond the garden gate.

"Good morning."

Gabriel's voice sent a rush of startled pleasure through her, along with a rush of memory at her subconscious yearnings. She blushed.

"Good morning," she said shyly, turning to catch his gaze lifting from her thighs in the jeans she'd put on with a T-shirt, something she hadn't worn in years, but that felt comfortable and right.

The way his expression flickered made her smooth an uncertain hand down her hip. "I thought we were just going to the showroom so it didn't matter what I wore."

"Small change of plan," he said with a humorless smile. He tsked as his phone buzzed in his hand. "The press release is out. This is turning into something I want to drop off that balcony." He held up the phone and nodded at the half wall she leaned against.

"What's the new plan?" She folded her arms, bracing herself.

"Apparently newlyweds go on something

called a honeymoon. I have been asked a thousand times where ours will take place."

A pulse of anticipatory heat struck her loins. She blushed even harder, with guilt, as if he could see into her filthy mind and know what she had imagined. Could tell what she longed for.

"What I said last night stands." His cheek ticked and he looked away, mouth tight. "But a week out of the public eye will give you time to get used to all this while the attention dies down."

He wasn't happy. She could tell and lowered her lashes, feeling like a burden.

"I'm s—"

His phone buzzed again and he swore. "I have to take this. They're packing for us. We'll leave shortly."

"Where are we going?"

"Safari." He swiped to accept his call.

"Safari! *Where?*"

"Africa. Where else do you go on safari?"

Eight hours later, his sound-barrier-defying jet landed them in Tanzania. They climbed aboard a helicopter for another hour, but it passed quickly as she kept her nose pressed to the glass, viewing herds of zebras and wildebeests, elephants and antelope and giraffes from above.

Then they were on the ground, traveling by Jeep, passing within a few hundred meters of more animals, pausing beside a waterhole where muddy hippos wallowed and yawned.

Their driver did most of the talking. Gabriel wore mirrored aviator sunglasses and stretched his arm behind her seat, both tense and relaxed. Each time she smiled in wonder at him, she found him watching her and her heart skipped and bounced in reaction.

He must think her so foolish, snapping her neck around as she tried to take it all in, but if she didn't immerse herself in the spectacle around them, she would grow too conscious of his thigh splayed near her own. Or the way she would only have to slide down a little in her seat to nestle into that space beneath his arm.

He had told her they were staying in a camp, but despite the grass-pressed mud walls and thatched roofs, the collection of buildings was as luxurious as his supersonic airplane. They were shown through the main lodge where a dining room was set with china and crystal. A sturdy suspension bridge took them across a wide, shallow stream where crocodiles lurked. Strange birdcalls followed them into the open air of their raised villa. It had three bedrooms, each with a bed canopied in mosquito netting and a deck with a view across the Serengeti.

As she watched the setting sun streak glorious magenta and scarlet, indigo and marigold across the horizon, she heard the noise of ice shifting in a bucket behind her. She turned to see Gabriel in the shadowed lounge behind her, heard him peel the foil from the bottle he held.

"Do you want to put the light on?" she asked.

"Not yet. You make an interesting optical illusion standing there so still. Like a black hole in the shape of a woman cut from a piece of painted paper."

It was an innocuous thing to say, but knowing he'd been looking at her again made wires of tension tighten inside her.

"I'd forgotten what a big place the world really is." She looked out again, watching the last of the light fade. "It's as noisy as the city here, but in a different way, which makes it seem quiet. I feel small and remote and I should probably be terrified to be so far from civilization, but I just feel…calm."

The cork popped.

She chuckled at the incongruous, yet perfect timing. "Maybe not that far from civilization."

"No," he agreed.

She had the feeling his efficient staff packed "civilization" for him the way anyone else remembered a toothbrush.

"We should take this to the plunge pool. Cool off before dinner," he suggested as she came in to take a glass.

"I'd love that. I feel all sweaty. I'll change and join you there."

Not ready to walk out in, essentially, a bra and panties, she chose a tankini. The bottoms were black short shorts, the top a formfitting print that tied behind her neck. Bright swirls of neon twisted over and under the cups, accentuating her bust.

The small pool was situated in a grotto-like private balcony off the master bedroom, which Gabriel was using. Four torches cast flickering light and left a citrus scent in the air that she suspected were meant to discourage insects. Gabriel was in the water, his arms stretched along the edges, hair wet and slicked back from his face.

She tiptoed down the steps into the cool water, sipped her champagne and set it on the edge. And wondered how awkward the next week would be, trying to make conversation with a man who expressed so little.

"You would think they would situate the pool so guests could watch the sun set," she murmured, seeing nothing but bush around them.

"The privacy allows for suits to be optional."

She snapped him a look and he chuckled.

"Your face is priceless. I'm wearing a suit." He stood in a rush of water so she could see the snug band of black.

Not *much* of a suit. The water trickled and slid in silvery trails down every glorious bronze plane and dent in his chiseled physique. A black arrow of hair disappeared into the low band and the fabric cupped—

She jerked her gaze off that bulge and quickly wet her dry throat with a gulp of champagne. She thought he chuckled again, but he turned away to fetch the bottle out of the bucket, which he'd left on the edge near the stairs. He waded across to top up her glass, then refilled his own and settled beside her.

But she sensed his tension.

"Are you angry that we had to come here?" she asked.

"I don't have to do anything." He turned his head to regard her. "Neither do you."

And just like that, she understood his tension was the same kind that gripped her—sexual.

"What if I want to?" It was her *honeymoon*.

He stretched out his arm, setting his glass on the edge and tipping back his head. His chest rose above the water as he took in a deep breath and let it out.

"Do you know where babies come from, Luli?"

"Oh, for— Is that a real question? Yes." She rolled her eyes.

"Being a virgin, I'll presume you're not on any sort of contraception?"

"I've heard of something called condoms?" she shot back facetiously, then buried her mouth against the rim of her glass, admitting, "I'm *curious*."

"Curious is fine." He abruptly gathered her, easily floating her in the water so she was sitting with her knees straddling his thighs. His hands sat against the crook where the tops of her thighs met her hips, hot palms branding her through the fabric of her short shorts. "I'm more than curious. I'm obsessed with finding out how high this fire between us might burn."

That fire was beginning to consume her now. "Okay," she breathed, leaning in.

His thumbs dug in at her hips.

"But slipups happen. I signed our marriage contract thinking you would provide me an heir. If you don't want children, I'm not going to force you, but I will need some. If you don't want them, we'll have to divorce at some point so I can marry someone else who does."

She sat back and bit her lip in consternation.

"You see? I wasn't entirely joking when I said you shouldn't give your virginity to the first man you marry. How involved do you want to get, knowing this marriage won't last?"

"What is my second husband likely to think if I show up a virgin? You're appalled and—"

"I'm not appalled. I'm recognizing that your inexperience makes you vulnerable."

"Then give me experience," she near cried. "I've never had a boyfriend, never done anything. Here I am married, on my honeymoon, and I get nothing? That's so *typical* of the way my life goes."

She started to shift off his lap, but his hands tightened. His cheekbones were like scraped granite, high and hard.

"Stay." His voice was harsh, but not angry. "Kiss me. Take what you want, then."

She wanted to ask if he meant it, but her voice was caught in her throat and her thoughts burned away in the flare of heat in his gaze.

His hands shifted, barely moved really, but the easing of his thumbs at the front of her hip bones and the subtle pressure of his fingertips against the swells over her butt urged her to lean forward.

She started to set her hands on his shoulders, realized she still held her half glass of champagne and put it on the edge. Then she set her hands against the tense muscles of his neck and kissed him.

She kissed him the way he had kissed her, with long slides of her mouth across his, lips parted so they could taste one another. He was delicious. Better than champagne. And the way he kissed her back was pure magic. She wanted to do this forever, mouth catching at mouth, easing away then sinking back to be devoured by him.

She couldn't get close enough. She shifted, arched under the slide of his hands up her back and—

Oh. She knew what that pressure was, startlingly hard against the tender flesh between her legs. She tensed in surprise, rising slightly as her thighs tried to close.

He didn't disguise the hunger in his expression, didn't flinch from the fact she knew he was aroused. He only quirked a brow in silent query. A tug between her shoulder blades released the tension of the tie behind her neck and relaxed the fabric across her breasts.

She instinctively caught at it, saw the passion in his eyes dim slightly at her reflexive modesty. He swallowed, nodded slightly.

She slowly let her hands drop, taking the front of her top with her.

Her breasts sat partially submerged, nipples thrusting in dark coral peaks above the surface.

For long moments, he simply stared, breath unsteady. Then he said, "I want to taste that."

His voice was a spell, drawing her to dig her fingers into the tendons across his shoulders and lift on her knees, glorying in the way his hands slid all the way to the backs of her thighs and steadied her. Encouraged her to arch and offer herself in a way that had always made her wonder if it could really be all that—

His mouth enclosed the tip in heat and she opened her mouth in a soundless scream. He wasn't gentle as he threw her into the inferno. He was scorching and greedy, filling her with the pound of her own heart so she rocked there gently in the water, hammered by pleasure as he sucked at her. Caught in a net of live wires that pulsed sensations into her loins.

Just when she thought she couldn't take any more, he moved to the other breast.

She speared her fingers through his damp hair, encouraged him to draw harder, only distantly aware that the noises she heard weren't from a jungle animal, but from the one inside her. She was pushing her backside into the hands that squeezed and roamed, and began to sink back down so she could feel that fierce pressure of him between her legs again.

"More?" he asked against her mouth.

"Yes," she moaned, and kissed him with flagrant passion, twining her arms around his neck and tilting her head for maximum submission to his kiss. She wanted him to know what he was doing to her and to keep doing it.

His arms hardened. He lifted her as he stood in a sluice of water, surprising her into gasping. He turned and sat her on the edge.

"How much more? Lie back and let me taste the rest of you?"

Wicked tingles raced from her face to her breasts and deep into the flesh protected by the shorts he began to peel off her hip. She didn't have it in her to be quite so blatant, but he helped her, leaning over and licking at her nipples again so she eased back and let him have his fill.

He picked up the part of the top that covered her stomach and lifted it, kissed her quivering abdomen while his other hand continued easing the shorts off her hips. By the time she had to pick up her hips so he could get them right off, she was screaming with anticipation.

She let her eyes drift shut then, "Oh!"

He poured the cool champagne across the tops of her legs, chuckling at the way she jumped before he leaned down to take a long and luscious taste into the crease of her thigh.

"Still with me?" he asked, sipping from her navel and petting the backs of his knuckles over the fine hairs protecting her most sensitive flesh.

If she could form words, she would tell him he could do whatever he wanted to her. She was a virgin at the dragon's mercy, trapped in his private lair, feeling the heat of his breath.

"Yes," she hissed.

"You're beautiful. So beautiful," he said huskily, wafting the words across her mound.

He shifted her thigh onto his shoulder and gently spread the slippery dampness of her response against the petals of her sex.

She made a noise of agony and tried to muffle it with the back of her wrist.

"Let me know you like it," he ordered.

"I do," she moaned, ready to beg if he didn't quit teasing.

His fingertip circled, knowing exactly what he was doing because he chuckled softly and said, "You do." Then the heat of the most intimate kiss arrived. He crooked her knee outward and took his time feasting on her, letting her bask in the sheer magnificence of the experience.

This, she thought, staring up at the star-speckled sky, feeling the hot night breeze sensually caressing her everywhere that he couldn't reach—*this* was luxury. She never wanted or needed anything else in the world except this.

His finger lightly probed, making her clench in reaction and intensifying the sensations.

"Hurt?" He withdrew.

"No. Please." She was panting and had to lick her lips.

His touch returned, making her throw her arm across her eyes and lift her hips as she groaned jaggedly. It was so good, so good, and he kept pleasuring her with unhurried caresses until she thought she would liquefy and disappear.

His intrusion deepened slightly, did something that made the pleasure sharpen and redouble. She bit down on her lip as he focused on delivering her past what she could bear and into a profound climax. She sobbed with abandonment as her stomach muscles contracted and her thighs quivered, the whole of her convulsing in glorious release.

Slowly he withdrew his touch and planted two gentle kisses on each of her inner thighs before he rose to kiss her still-trembling abdomen.

"I have to go shower. Now." His voice grated with strain. "Before I forget my good intentions and take this too far."

She rolled her head on the hard tiles beneath her, still filled with lassitude. "I'd like to touch you. Help."

"Do you realize what's going to happen if you do?"

"In theory." She smiled with her newfound womanly experience. "That's why I want to do it."

He made a noise that was both strangled laughter and defeat. In a lithe move, he settled beside her on the tiles and covered her mouth, kissing her with all the passion in him that had yet to be satisfied.

It made her hungry again and she kissed him with abandon until he growled with suffering. She cupped his jaw, urging him to back off a little so she could see.

His tiny bathing suit was too small to contain his arousal. Fascinated, she started to reach out, glanced at him.

"Be my guest."

"Show me," she whispered.

He did, wrapping her hand around him and teaching her what he liked. They kissed again as she caressed him. Kissed until the hand he'd tangled in her hair stung and his body shuddered and his feral cries spilled across her lips.

They enjoyed a mellow dinner in the dining room, chatting on and off with the couple at the next table.

Luli almost felt as though Gabriel had deliberately drawn those other people in to dispel the intimacy between him and Luli, which stung. She was beginning to realize what he'd meant about how she needed to be careful how much of herself she gave him. He had warned her that physical closeness would make her long for the emotional kind and it was true. She already did.

What she didn't understand was why he didn't want to give it to her.

"Can I ask why you were estranged from Mae?" She paused on the bridge to take hold of the rope that formed the rails and looked up at the stars. "I know she didn't exactly reach out. She was very reserved. Is that a family trait?" she tacked on lightly.

"To some extent." He moved to stand beside her. "I don't spend a lot of time navel-gazing and paying therapists to tell me my family of origin is the source of all my problems, but what little I remember of my mother, she was very quiet. Regretful, perhaps, but I may be projecting. Given that Mae drove my mother to marry my father, I didn't see a point in pursuing a relationship with her and possibly winding up committing a similar act of recklessness."

"Present marriage excluded."

"Of course."

She smiled briefly, but it faded to sadness. "Your parents weren't in love?" Was that why he didn't feel he was capable of it? He had no example of it?

"My father was. Perhaps my mother was." What she could see of his shadowed expression was inscrutable. "I don't remember them fighting, but I was young."

"How did she die? Mae never said."

"A complication with her pregnancy. She wouldn't let them take the baby and they both died."

"I'm so sorry. That's terrible." She thought of Mae's inexpressive face on the few occasions when she had mentioned her daughter. She must have been containing so much pain.

Much like Gabriel's mask of indifference as he nodded toward the end of the bridge where their villa sat.

She didn't take the hint.

"You lost a brother or sister." He must be terribly lonely.

His shoulder jerked. "I wouldn't wish my childhood on anyone else."

She cocked her head, thinking of what he'd said about being bullied. "Mixed race? I thought America was the great melting pot, accepting of all."

"What does that even mean?" he scoffed. "I'm pig iron, that's true, but I wasn't something anyone had use for until I refined myself into that other American ideal, the self-made man." He spoke with an infinite depth of cynicism.

"I hate that feeling of not fitting." Her heart panged with more than empathy. She was living that feeling even now. "The pageant school was a competitive place, but at least we all looked and sounded the same. The whole time I've been at Mae's, I've felt like a big, sore thumb. Now I'm with you and I'm a square peg trying to fit into a dollar sign."

"Fitting in is overrated."

"I do that." In so many ways, they were so alike. "I convince myself I don't want what I can't have."

His resounding silence made her look up at him. He seemed so remote in that moment, her heart lurched.

"What I mean is, I always told myself it didn't matter that I didn't have money of my own because my needs were always met," she tried to explain. "It works as a coping strategy. Especially when I looked at all the money Mae had and she didn't have what she really wanted, which was her daughter."

Still he said nothing.

"I'm not saying you're wrong," she hurried on. "Mae *was* difficult. I presumed she was controlling and isolated me because she had lost her daughter, but it wouldn't surprise me if that was her nature from the beginning. Maybe your mother felt suffocated and pushed Mae away. I wouldn't think your mother giving birth to you was an act of defiance, though. She probably wanted a family. If she had survived and you had siblings, you maybe wouldn't have felt so set apart."

"It's late. We should both get some sleep." He touched her shoulder.

She hesitated. "Together?"

"I don't think that's wise." His flinty gaze met hers, read the injury she couldn't hide. "I did warn you," he said of his gentle rebuff.

If this was how much it hurt to be close to him, then pushed away, he was right. It was too much to bear. More than she wanted to risk.

Forlorn, she went to bed alone.

He didn't hear her so much as feel her move through the villa as sunrise approached. He rose from the bed where his mind had been too noisy and his body on fire with the knowledge he could have her—he only needed to compromise what few principles he had.

He had taken things way too far by the plunge pool, rationalizing that he was doing a damned public service by granting her the experience she craved.

He had pushed the boundaries, though.

He had seduced her and had wanted all that they'd done and more. *Everything.* He was quite convinced she would have gone all the way if he'd guided her there.

Her startled newness to his most intimate caresses had told him she was as virginal as she claimed, however, passionate response notwithstanding. Recognizing that had allowed him to keep his head and take her to dinner instead of keeping her under him the rest of the night.

When she appeared dressed for dinner wearing a dreamy, adoring smile, he had realized his arrogant mistake. He had spent the next hours backpedaling, not wanting to lead her on.

Because he wasn't like other people. He might meet society's expectations by marrying and producing heirs, but only because he saw the elegant simplicity in it. He didn't want or need a wife and family. He wasn't trying to "fit in" or feel closer to anyone.

I do that. Convince myself I don't want what I can't have.

Her words shouldn't stick like a fishbone in his throat, but they did. He was an honest person, especially with himself. And he had always known himself to prefer being alone.

At least, he had managed to convince himself he preferred living solo. It wasn't lost on him that he was clinging to that belief even as he stood here watching her instead of lying alone in his bed.

She wore a pair of loose pajama bottoms and a snug, sleeveless top. She took a moment to look out at the western horizon, still purple and dotted with fading stars, then looked to the moon.

No. She was orienting herself.

She took up a stance facing north and rubbed her palms together, taking her time, taking in the world around her, taking a few deep breaths. Then she slowly drew her hands apart, fingers relaxed. She began to shape an invisible ball.

Chi.

He set his own palms together and began working up his own energy sphere as he walked out in his boxers and joined her.

She glanced at him, but neither said anything. He had taken the odd class in many different martial arts over the years, but hadn't done tai chi in a long time. Even so, it was easy to follow her fluid movement when she stepped her feet apart and began. As she turned west and moved so gracefully, her forms could have been mistaken for a modern ballet, but each move was as much a practice of self-defense as his own lightning-fast kung fu.

He matched his breathing to hers, mirroring the care she took as she moved in and out of block and protect, retreat and strike, gather chi, shield, jab and push, draw in again.

Did he notice the elegant line of her spine? The thrust of her breasts and the curve of her ass as she lunged? Yes. It filled him with sexual vigor and admiration for nature's ability to create perfection. It made him strive all the harder to execute each turn and press as precisely as possible, exactly as she did.

East now. Jab to chest while opponent is down. Twist. Perfectly synchronized, as if they'd been doing this all their lives, they spread crane wings and crept down with one leg extended, like a snake. His mind was filled with everything and nothing, thoughts flitting through to stick or fall as they would. He lived inside his muscles, his bones, his organs, aware of the slide of his blood in his arteries and the air exchanging in his lungs.

And just as his warmed hands had formed a ball of energy after he rubbed them together and held them apart, a similar force of *chi* grew in the space between them. As their bodies warmed and their breath soughed in measured hisses, his life force picked up hers and grew into something bigger, unseen, yet tangible. Energy swirled between them like ocean currents and trade winds and molten lava deep in the earth's core.

This was what it would be like to make love to her. Pure Zen. For a moment, he imagined this feeling could permeate a whole life together.

But that was an illusion. Another attempt to rationalize the sex he ached for. He'd seen the hurt in her expression last night. He couldn't ignore how vulnerable she was beneath that veneer of mouthwatering beauty and heart-stopping bravery.

She pivoted them north for the final scoop, bring feet together, fist into palm and close with a bow.

With his bent body, he thanked her for the practice and he thanked her for the teaching. He was not a man without cravings, only a man who pretended not to have them. But satisfying those cravings at the expense of someone else would put a weight on his soul.

So he would not, and could not, satisfy his craving for her. He would exercise discipline and resist.

He straightened and went directly to the chill waters of the plunge pool.

CHAPTER EIGHT

LULI FROWNED WHEN she logged in and saw a balance had dropped significantly lower than she expected. She popped into the account and gasped.

"You're in!" She flashed a look at Gabriel, lounging indolently on the sofa across from her, feet on the ottoman, his own laptop on his thighs. His amused gaze hit hers.

"Since last night. Took you long enough to notice."

"I haven't had a chance, have I?" They'd been on the savanna all day, then swam and ate and finally settled in with their devices a few minutes ago.

She closed the lid of her laptop, setting it aside. "Congratulations?" she offered.

His brows moved in an infinitesimal acknowledgment, unimpressed with his own prowess. Given this was how he made his living, she had expected him to outmaneuver her very quickly, but she still craved an acknowledgment of the effort it took him to do it. She wanted him to see her as a laudable opponent.

And she desperately needed to know, "What now?"

He already held all the power between them. Even the sexual supremacy. It didn't seem to matter if they were half-naked in the plunge pool, moving within inches of each other through the forms of tai chi or sitting like this, feet almost sole to sole. He indicated no more than casual awareness of her while she was in a constant state of heightened senses. His scent, the heat off his body, the husk of his laugh. It all made her thirst for *more*.

Consent went both ways, she kept telling herself morosely.

His cheeks hollowed. "Come tell me what's going on here." He nodded at his screen.

She moved to perch next to him. "Oh. I didn't agree with Mae on this, but she had a longtime relationship with that company."

Thirty minutes of discussion followed on a handful of other funds and transactions in Mae's portfolio. Gabriel had a higher risk tolerance than Mae, which made Luli feel defensive about the decisions she had made in the past.

Gabriel watched her mouth while she spoke, which distracted her. They were spending nearly every waking minute together. Which was the point of a honeymoon, she supposed, but married couples usually exorcised this tension with sex. Her desire for him was making it nearly impossible to respond to his incisive questions.

She finally sat back with her hands in her lap. By this time she had her knees folded beneath her and was facing him on the sofa.

"I have to know, Gabriel. Are you going to lock me out? I really like doing this."

"I can tell," he said, not mocking her. "And some of my Ivy League executives aren't putting this much analysis and consideration into their decisions. I can't run all these as separate entities for any length of time, though. It's not practical."

"You're firing me?"

"Consider yourself on notice. Keep doing what you're doing for the moment, but discuss all your decisions with me. I'll start breaking this into pieces and farming them out once we're back in New York and I can meet with some of my people."

"You just said I'm good at it!"

"No, I said you're thorough and careful. You're micromanaging, which has its drawbacks."

"You're going to fire me because I *care*? What am I supposed to do if I don't do this?

"Be a society wife?"

"Ha-ha. You don't want a wife. Not me, anyway. Is that why you're planning to fire me from that, too?" she asked on a sudden burst of understanding that his rejection had nothing to do with whether she wanted children. "Because I care too much?"

He turned his head, expression a dark glower. "Yes."

Crushed and trying not to show it, she shifted to sit straight, knees hugged to her chest. Her mind reached and tried to grasp, but only found thin air.

"Luli." He sighed. His elbow nudged hers. "I care enough to want to look after you. Don't worry about whether you're working."

"I want to look after myself," she muttered, feet hitting the floor in a stomp. "Of course I'm going to worry about it."

"Where are you going?" he asked as she started toward the door.

"Where any society wife goes when her husband tells her to quit her job and stay home. To spend his money at the nearest shop."

"If you come back wearing zebra print, I'll divorce you on the spot."

"I'll buy them out, then." She swung the door shut behind her.

Disappointing a woman was not new territory for him. Feeling like an ass about it was. Gabriel stood by what he had said, though. It wasn't practical to keep her running a separate entity, double-checking and doubting herself, simply to give her something to do. Granted, she'd never been given the chance to take full responsibility. In time, she might prove to be more assertive and successful, but he'd find something else for her to cut her teeth on.

In the meantime, he half expected her to lock him out of Mae's accounts again—or at least try. He plugged all the holes she'd found in his code, but she was wily.

Apparently she wasn't the type to hold a grudge, though. She came back from the gift shop with a bar of specialty chocolate and offered him some.

"I'll find something for you," he promised her.

"I don't want nepotism. No one would respect me—including me." She popped a square into her mouth, chewed thoughtfully. "All I knew was beauty pageants until I worked for Mae. Education is never wasted, but sometimes you need more despite what you have. I'll figure out the next stage for myself. You don't have to give me a job just to make me feel useful."

He respected that desire for independence, but still wanted to look after her. It was a tough line to walk. He really wished he could see her as an employee or a project or an exotic creature he could pet and play with and ultimately set free with smug satisfaction at having rescued and rehabilitated her.

But there was no hiding the fact she was a woman, even when she dressed like a man.

He took her to the office with him when they landed in New York. She was still caretaking Mae's investments and he had some ideas on how to utilize her skills, but he needed to put a few more pieces in place first.

Mostly he brought her with him because he couldn't stand the idea of leaving her alone in his penthouse all day. Which was all about her, he chided himself. *He* could have gone those hours without seeing her just fine.

With equal parts curiosity and wariness, she took her cue from his custom-made suit and dressed in flared pants with a matching pinstriped vest over a crisp white shirt with a sharply pointed collar. She twisted her hair up and carried a briefcase that cost as much as the sleek new laptop within it. She rather cheekily pilfered one of his ties and wore it loose enough her collar exposed the hollow in the base of her throat.

She was sexy as hell. If anything, the contrast of authoritative masculine clothes on her nonstop curves made her femininity more obvious. Very much more alluring.

After a week of trying to ignore her round ass in snug khakis and the way perspiration gathered between her breasts in her low, round-necked undershirts, it was taking all his concentration to behave like a civilized man when the territorial beast inside him wanted so badly to *mate*.

But he couldn't. He didn't know how he would keep his control in place, but he would.

They turned heads as he walked her through his top-floor offices.

"That's the meeting I left when I got your message." He thumbed toward a glass wall into a boardroom where a dozen faces, stern and concerned and curious, watched them walk past. "Come find me if you need me. I'll be there for a few hours."

He continued along to the open door of the office closest to his own.

"Luli, this is Marco."

"Sir." The good-looking, well-dressed Latino man stopped typing and stood. He was a little older than Luli and eyed her with sharp interest as he came around to greet them. "Congratulations on your recent marriage, sir. And thank you for the promotion. I appreciate your thinking of me."

He shook Gabriel's hand and smiled warmly at Luli as he shook hers. "Mrs. Dean, welcome."

"Nice to meet you," Luli murmured shyly, gaze taking in the view of Central Park behind the sleek desk, the mini fridge beneath the bar and the presentation screen over the meeting table with four chairs. "I'll set up there and check in with Singapore while you're tied up?" she suggested to Gabriel, nodding at the table.

God, she was adorable.

"Luli, we've talked about this," he admonished sternly, enjoying her discomfiture as she widened her eyes and grew defensive.

"I want to make those transfers we talked about on the plane. You said I should continue doing what I was doing until you made other arrangements."

"Do your work at your desk. This is your office." He moved so she could see the plate on the door read Lucrecia Dean. "Marco has everything set up for you. He's your personal assistant. If you need anything—thumbtacks, dry cleaning, tickets to a Broadway show— he'll source it. But make sure I'm free to go with you. Sync our calendars," he told Marco.

"Done, sir."

"Thank you. Marco speaks Spanish," Gabriel added to Luli. "It's one of the reasons I thought he'd be a good fit for you."

"I barely do," she admitted sheepishly to Marco. "It's been such a long time." She pushed her mouth to the side in a look that was both reproving and rueful as she realized Gabriel had been deliberately teasing her, letting her think Marco was her boss or sitter. *Gracias.*

"*De nada.* We have plans tonight. Steal a nap on the sofa in my office if you need it." Unable to resist, he kissed her cheek before he walked out.

Wear something dramatic, Gabriel had said when he informed her they would attend a black-tie gala benefiting a museum.

The gown Luli chose was made of stretch lace with subtle dragons embroidered into it. It clung to her arms and flared out at the hem to create the impression ink had been poured down her body and splashed out around her feet. It was lined with nude satin so she wore only a peach-colored thong beneath. The plunging neckline didn't allow for a bra and she applied double-sided tape against her cleavage to avoid a slip.

Her shoes were a glamorous half dozen straps bedecked with rhinestones and a high ankle strap. She straightened her hair to a sleek curtain combed back from her face then drew attention to her eyes with mauve and gold, chartreuse and teal. Her lips received a coat of dark red called Salem.

"Are you trying to kill me?" Gabriel stopped with his drink halfway to his mouth when she appeared.

"Really?" She smiled with shy pleasure and gave him the one-hand-on-her-hip pose. A small weight shift and she changed hands, giving her hair a slow flip along the way, so the curtain gently spilled off the back of her hand. She held her pose, chin high, gaze on the distant future, not a care in the world.

"You're going to put the entire city in the hospital." He pretended to take a phone call. "Yeah, that was my wife. I can't help it if she's that freaking hot. Get a better power grid because she's going to keep knocking it out."

She burst out laughing, flattered, but more bowled over that he would be so silly about it. It helped her relax and pin a smile of lingering humor on her face when they arrived at the chaotic zoo that was the red carpet.

An audible "Whoa…" rose from the crowd. Photographers hurried into position to snap their photo, demanding to know who she was wearing and how was her honeymoon and when had they started dating.

Gabriel drew her inside before she had to answer.

"Are there specific people you need to see tonight?" Luli asked as he handed her a flute of champagne. She wanted to be prepared and help in any way she could, not run away with a case of stage fright this time.

"They'll come to us," he said with careless arrogance. His eyes narrowed as she released a small snort. "What?"

"I'm wondering if you ever go to anyone." After seeing him in several environments now, she was realizing she wasn't the only one in awe of him. From janitor to pilot to executive to governor, people fell over themselves trying to anticipate his needs.

"Not if I can help it," he answered unabashedly. "I hate people. I only talk to them if they make me."

"Hmmph." She hollowed her cheeks and looked across the crowd.

"You don't count," he said.

"Because I'm not a person," she surmised.

She studied the tiara of a matron who passed them. Luli wore a pair of teardrop diamond earrings Gabriel had given her before they left. She hadn't wanted to accept them, but he had said they were a loan—unless she decided to keep them. Which she wouldn't. But she loved them and wished she could.

"Luli." His tone was apologetic. He touched her arm.

She let him see that she was laughing beneath her mask of affront.

He tsked and sipped, profile filling with self-disgust as he turned his face away.

Why that was funny, she didn't know, but it was. She laughed with open enjoyment and he looked at her with so much admiration, he melted her bones and made every other part of her sing. He was so handsome, he hurt her eyes. His chiseled face and keen stare, his barely-there hint of a cynical smile, his mussed hair that she wanted to muss even more, lingering over the feel of those fine strands between her fingers…

Save yourself for a relationship that matters. Someone special.

Did he not realize *he* was special?

"Gabriel!" A woman appeared beside him and snaked her touch around his arm, smooshing her breasts against his elbow. "Introduce me to your wife."

"Brittany Farris," he said after a brief pause. "Lucrecia Dean."

Brittany offered air kisses and *had* to know *everything* about how they had met.

Luli had met variations of this woman before. Some girls on the pageant circuit were genuinely nice—and scared to be on their own. They did everything they could to make friends, needing bolstering and the safety of numbers. Some, like Luli, were there to win. They weren't mean, but they didn't make friends because feelings got hurt and friendships folded when there could be only one winner.

Then there were these kind—the ones who acted like friends, but didn't have a nice bone in their bodies.

"Luli managed my grandmother's business affairs for the last eight years," Gabriel explained.

"I saw the headlines about your inheritance! You're a *trillionaire*!" Her excitement was quickly schooled into a pout of sympathy. "But I'm so sorry, of course. I didn't even know you had a grandmother, let alone a raging romance with her *business manager*." She gave Luli a once-over. "You must be *very* shrewd if you've kept this relationship under wraps all this time."

Luli did what she had done with every other witch who thought she could backhand her with a compliment.

"Gabriel called me cunning the other day, didn't you?"

Over the rim of his glass, he asked her if that was really how she wanted to play this, as if he didn't think she understood who she was dealing with.

"I did," he admitted after a beat. "And I meant it."

Someone else came up, forcing Brittany on her way. Gabriel held court for the rest of the evening, continuing to introduce her as Mae's manager even when a professor from a prestigious design school asked if Luli had ever considered modeling, providing the perfect opportunity to talk about her pageant experience.

Gabriel squeezed her hand, however, warning her to demur.

"Every tall girl is told they must model or play basketball, aren't they?" she said.

"Not every girl is told as vehemently as

I'm telling *you*. I have contacts at several agencies. Gabriel, she needs to be immortalized in the pages of *Vogue*, wearing Chanel. You can't let these cheekbones languish in an office."

"Why not? Mine do," Gabriel said with blithe conceit. "Luli is one of the best programmers I've come across. I'll fight to keep her."

She couldn't tell if he was being sincere, but the man moved on and other people moved in.

"You've been quiet," Gabriel said a few hours later, when they arrived back at his penthouse. "Was it too much?"

"No," she murmured. "It was just a long night of being 'on.' My face hurts from smiling."

"Don't feel you have to. I don't."

She had read that memo in his expression of bored tolerance.

She'd seen his home earlier so she wasn't as agog returning to it, but was still taken aback that he lived in this massive split-level mansion in the sky. The foyer led to a sunken lounge where the exterior wall held another of his spectacular aquariums. It formed the inside wall of the infinity pool outside—which looked down onto Central Park.

She lowered to the sofa, its cushion stuffed with goose down, he had informed her, when her first time sitting caused her to gasp with a sense of sinking into pure luxury. All of his furniture was custom-made for him by an Italian couture house that hand-turned legs and hand-stitched pleats into leather and velvet.

They measure me like my tailor, even ask me which side I dress, he'd drawled.

One of his servants appeared with a pot of Chinese tea, something she had confessed to craving after her breakdown in Paris. It appeared every night now, without her asking for it.

"Thank you," she said with a warm smile for the maid.

The woman curtsied.

Luli sighed. *I'm one of you,* she wanted to say, but Gabriel dismissed her.

"I thought Brittany might have said something to upset you," he said as the door closed. He shrugged out of his jacket and loosened his tie, throwing both on the back of the sofa, gaze staying fixed on her.

"When?" She set aside her shoes and wiggled her toes with relief. Then she picked up her skirt as she walked across to where the tea had been left on the bar.

"She came out of the ladies' room after you did and smiled at me like she had sunk my battleship."

"Please." Luli glanced over her shoulder so he could see her brow crinkled with scorn and pity. "I know a school in Venezuela where she could learn to be a cat with actual claws."

"So she did say something." His voice tightened.

"She told me you slept together." She paused in pouring, glanced at him again and saw by his tense expression that it was true. She ignored the fresh strip that admission peeled off the back of her heart. "Actually, she asked whether *you* had told me that you'd been lovers." She finished pouring and set the pot aside. "I said you probably didn't think it was important enough to mention."

He looked away, but even in the subdued lighting she saw the twitch of his mouth.

"Then she warned me that she could blackball me among the social elite here. I told her I'd never heard the expression, but that she must feel very disappointed things hadn't worked out between you, and maybe it was because she talked about you behind your back." One spoon of sugar. "I said I'd ask you. She didn't like that."

She heard his snort.

"Then I told her I would look up *blackball* so I understood *exactly* how that works." Her spoon clinked as she stirred.

He swore under his breath, head hanging and shoulders shaking. "Every time I worry about you, I discover you're perfectly capable of taking care of yourself."

"Are *you*?" she asked, facetious, but also with tendrils of jealousy still working its poison through her veins in thorny little stings. "Why would you sleep with someone like that? What happened to saving it for someone special?"

"I'm not a virgin."

She turned fully around to see his hands had balled in his pockets. His jaw had hardened. All of him had.

"Is it easier to remain celibate when you know what you're missing?" A horrifying thought occurred. "Have you been seeing someone while we've been—?"

"No! When would I even— We're together *all the time*. I have been celibate since we met and no, it is not easy."

"Then… How long does this marriage have to last, Gabriel? Are we supposed to wait to have sex until it's over?"

"What are you asking? Whether you're allowed to have sex with other people? No. Neither of us is stepping out. It's gossip we don't need and would jeopardize the believability of this marriage."

"So I'm just supposed to live here with you, wondering what sex would be like?"

He closed his eyes and sounded very beleaguered. "I've told you why we shouldn't have sex."

"Because you might hurt my feelings when this is over. Well, I'll tell you what. It hurts my feelings that you'd have sex with someone like *her* and can't bring yourself to make love to *me*."

"Brittany? That's what this is about?" He shoved a hand into his hair. "People want things from me, Luli. All the time." He spoke with the infinite weariness of a battle-scarred warrior. "Sometimes it seems simpler to sleep with someone who is transparent in their motives. I didn't realize how much she drinks or I wouldn't have gone near her. It lasted less than a week."

He had said his father drank himself to death. She wanted to ask how bad it had been, but the remote cloud around him told her it had been very bad. Her heart tremored, urging her to go to him, but his stillness held her off.

"I don't drink," she pointed out. "No more than you do."

"I've noticed. I appreciate it."

"So…?"

"Luli. You're far too vulnerable."

"You just said you don't have to worry about me."

"Yet I do."

"Well, I'm worried about you! You have sex with people you don't even *like*."

"That was one misjudgment. Just…give it a rest," he sighed. "We can't, okay? I can't let you start thinking this is real."

"How is having sex making this more or less real? People who are married have sex. You're afraid that if we sleep together, I'm going to want you to fall in love with me?"

"Yes."

She folded her arms, aching because she already wanted that. Her marriage already looked very bleak, filled with lust and craving and deep yearning while he felt…nothing.

"I can't say I wouldn't," she admitted. "I've always wanted someone to love me."

His expression tightened as if her words had scored a line through him. "It's not as idyllic as it sounds, trust me."

"How do you know? Have you loved someone?" The world tilted and nearly dropped her off the edge into cold, airless space. "Is that why—"

"No," he said, taking her aback with his harsh tone.

"No? Not even your parents?"

"Of course my mother." He sounded like she was yanking out his teeth.

"Not 'of course.' I have no feelings for my father and terrible ones toward my mother. If you loved your mother and she loved you back, that's good."

"Well, I have grief over the loss of my mother, because I *loved* her. And terrible feelings toward my father. He couldn't handle her loss *at all*. It was a nightmare. Because he *loved* her. He railed and wept and broke things. He told me love was agony and never to let myself feel it."

For once Gabriel had stepped outside his jaded, impervious shell. He was breathing fire, snarling and showing his claws.

"I wouldn't bother taking the advice of a man who was drunk and slurring from ten in the morning on," he continued, "but he would grab me and cry against my chest, fall to his knees and tell me he loved *me*. He made me promise never to leave, never to get hurt or get sick or die. I was seven. I didn't know how to promise that! And I don't know if I loved him, but I do know it was agony."

Oh, Gabriel. She swallowed, thinking of

him being confused and grieving, then picked on at school. So alone.

Until he had money. Then everyone wanted to be his friend.

She abandoned her tea and went across to him, took off her earrings and made him give her his hand so she could put them in his palm.

"I love these. They're beautiful. But I don't want to keep them unless you want me to have them. You've given me things I *need*, Gabriel. You've given me someone who listens and draws me a bath and calls me intelligent. That's far more valuable to me than anything you could buy me."

She closed his fingers over the earrings, then ran her thumb across the hard bumps of his knuckles. She wanted to kiss his fist, which felt silly and too impactful. Emotions suffused her that she didn't know how to express. There was gratitude, definitely, but other nameless things that urged her to reach out and offer, search for something in him, but give up to him at the same time.

"I have nothing to give you that equals any of that." Her voice creaked.

His mouth opened in protest, but she squeezed his hand.

"Only me," she continued. "And I *want* to.

It's okay if you don't love me. But I want to touch you and hold you and feel those things you make me feel. I want to know what it might feel like if someone *did* love me."

His breath hissed in and he pulled his hand from her touch, thrusting his closed fist into his pocket.

She set her hand on his chest. "I don't want you to protect me from you or myself. I want you to let me become the woman *I* want to be."

He made a strangled noise and pinched the bridge of his nose, eyes clenched shut.

"Please?"

"I'm only a man, Luli," he said in a rasping voice. "When this all goes to hell, I want you to remember this moment. I tried to be honorable."

CHAPTER NINE

"REALLY?" EXCITEMENT AND TREPIDATION and anticipation all came together in a war inside her.

"I've been wanting to tear that gown off you all night." He opened his eyes and there was such atavistic light in his gaze, her heart stuttered.

"Don't! I love it." She looked down at her cleavage. "Plus there's tape that will sting so bad if you pull it too fast."

"You were put on this earth to drive me crazy. Go. Lock yourself in your room or meet me in mine. *Now.*"

She picked up her skirt and ran up the stairs, hearing him take them two at a time behind her. She let out a wild laugh, riding an adrenaline rush. She went straight to his room where she whirled to confront him.

He came in behind her, shirt open and pulled from his tuxedo pants, edges wafting like wings.

She gasped in awe at the sheen of his burnished skin stretched taut across lean muscles. He stalked her on panther feet and grasped her hips, dragging her into a soft collision with his bare chest. His mouth came down on hers in a blatant claim of ownership. His lips were hard. Devouring. Insatiable.

Her body responded in a flowering throb that made all of her hurt. She moaned at the pleasure-pain of it and he immediately dragged his head up.

"No?" he asked through gritted teeth.

"Yes," she breathed. Groaned. She tangled her hands in his hair exactly as she had wanted to and urged him back to kissing her. She pressed her tongue to his and cried out with excitement when he sucked on her.

Wet, fiery kisses went down her to her throat. His arms folded all the way around her narrow waist and he held her tight and still, teeth against the straining cord in her neck.

"Tell me you want this," he said against her skin. "Because I'm barely hanging on to control."

"I do. So much." She pushed her hands beneath his open shirt, freeing his shoulders, wanting to touch all of him.

He straightened to throw off his shirt and she saw his eyes, feral and ravenous. It sent a dangerous spire of hunger into the pit of her belly. Lower. Liquid heat pooled between her legs and she clenched with emptiness and longing.

"Take it off, then." He nodded at her dress.

She swallowed and ran her fingertips along the inner swells of her breasts, watching him watch her lift the strap off her skin. She turned and gathered her hair onto the front of her shoulder, revealing the zipper at her spine.

He released it. Slowly. The lace relaxed and his hot hands took possession of her bared waist. He kissed the top of her spine and his humid breath fogged near her ear.

"The way you smell drives me insane. I want to lick every inch of you." His teeth nipped her lobe and her nipples tightened so hard and fast, they stung. She pressed her thighs tight together, trying to ease the ache that shot high and hot between.

She eased the dress down off her shoulders, but before she had it fully off her arms, his hands stole forward to claim her breasts. She stilled, head falling back against his shoulder as he fondled her, filling her with lassitude. Her backside instinctively pressed into the firmness behind his fly and his breath hissed at the way she writhed against him. His hands tightened on her and she felt his teeth again, scraping the tender place where her neck met her shoulder.

"Keep going," he demanded, pushing into her butt, confusing her a little when he added, "I want to see you."

She kept herself snug against his fly as she turned her sleeves inside out peeling them off. He stepped back then, just enough to let her push the clingy dress off her hips. She stepped out of it and turned.

His gaze claimed her in a lazy exploration that was nearly tactile, taking his time and leaving a burn of awareness at each curve and swell. He only held her one hand in his own, wasn't even squeezing, but somehow he kept her in place for his leisurely inspection. His free hand came out and his finger hooked into her thong at the hollow on the front of her hip.

And finally, his gaze lifted to meet hers.

She only licked her lips, waiting. His heavy touch eased the one side down her hip, then skimmed across, grazing her mound on the way.

She jerked and the corners of his mouth deepened with satisfaction. He slid the other side down an inch, teased her again with the back of his knuckle against the humid seam of her folds.

"Gabriel," she whispered in a helpless throb.

"Is this what you want?" The thong cut across the tops of her thighs while his touch traveled back to center and barely touched her, petting ever so lightly.

She bit her lip, embarrassed by the release of moisture there, but so wanting him to stroke into it.

"Say yes."

"Yes," she obeyed in a thready voice.

He traced the center line of her, slowly deepening the caress, driving her mad so she was biting her lips, eyes clenched tight, waiting and waiting.

There.

Her mouth opened in a soundless scream as he found the swollen knot of nerves that craved his touch.

He made a noise that was a growl of satisfaction and a snarl of torment.

"Please," she whispered and blindly reached out.

"You're okay." He stepped closer, folding her arm behind the small of her back as he kept her hand in his and embraced her. Held her up. His other hand kept torturing her while his mouth found hers. "Feel," he said against her lips, and continued his delicious torture.

She curled her free hand around his neck and kissed him back, lost in a sea of sensation as he dragged his mouth across hers and her twisting scraped her nipples against the hair on his chest. And his hand, oh, his wicked, masterful hand found a wonderful rhythm that she met with abbreviated thrusts of her hips.

She tried to tell him she wanted him, all of him, filling that ache. She wanted that hard shape she could feel so implacably against her hip, but she was drowning in this kiss and the pleasure and suddenly she was showered in the spell of climax, shivering and clinging and gasping.

And Gabriel was laughing softly. "I knew," he said against her lips. "I knew we would be like this."

She went bonelessly onto his bed like a gift. Her hair pooled in ribbons of brunette satin, framing her face. Her gaze was soft, her mouth pouted and swollen from their kisses. Her limbs splayed weightlessly and her curves beckoned.

His mouth watered as he stripped the last of his clothes. Somehow he remembered a condom when the only thought in his head was that he had to be against her. Over her.

In her. He noted the hint of apprehension as she watched, studying his engorged shape, and knew he would die if he had to wait.

But wait he would. As long as it took.

He settled over her and cupped her face, letting himself burn in the fire of need and craving and anticipation of relief. When he kissed her, he tasted hesitation. He felt the tension in her thighs as she nervously made room for him.

He kissed her chin, the heavy but slow pulse in her throat. She wasn't nearly as frantic as he wanted her. Her collarbone, so delicate, reminded him that all of her was fragile, whether she realized it or not.

Ah, these breasts. They were a fantasy unto themselves and he gave himself free rein to pleasure both of them, teasing and sucking and licking until her nipples were turgid beads against his tongue.

"Gabriel," she gasped. The fingers in his hair began to clench with desperation, but she wasn't yet near the level gripping him.

"Soon," he soothed, drawn by her scent to rub his face across the trembling muscles in her abdomen and here. *Here* was the magic and the sweetness and the way to fully prepare her for the hard thrusts of his body.

He tantalized, glorying in the honeyed perfection of her until she moved without inhibition, making exquisitely helpless noises that shredded his control. He longed to take her over the edge like this, but she was in such a delicious state of surrender.

Now, finally, her body held the same frequency of tremble, the same throbbing agony of desire that echoed his own.

He rose over her and braced himself on an elbow while he sought her center. Somehow he made himself command, "Say it again." He had to know they were perfectly aligned.

"Yes," she told him, eyes opening to slits that were glazed with passion. "I need you. Please."

He tried to be gentle. She was tight and the heel of her hand pressed into his shoulder. She caught her breath. He stopped. Gritted his teeth.

"It's okay," she murmured, biting her lip as she shifted.

He withdrew a fraction. Kissed her. Slowly she relaxed and feathered a caress in the base of his spine.

He let his weight sink the rest of him into her, all the way, until his eyes nearly rolled to the back of his head with sheer ecstasy.

Mine, he thought, knowing that to think it

was to take something from her, but in this moment it felt like a fair exchange.

Because she possessed him. Utterly and completely.

Luli was trembling in what she thought might be shock, but Gabriel lifted his head and just that tiny shift of movement caused such a wave of heated pleasure to wash over her, her scalp tingled and she was suddenly on the verge of climax again.

This was acute arousal holding her in its grip, she realized. She was quivering with desire.

Her loins stung where he intruded, but she loved it. *Needed* it. Restless frustration guided her hands as she ran them over his back and hips, claiming tense muscles and hot, damp skin.

He kissed her, the rake of his mouth drugging, but inciting. Her knees lifted on instinct, ankles crossing in the small of his back.

He made an animalistic noise and sank a fraction deeper into her. Then he gathered her beneath him, withdrew slowly and returned in a steady thrust, all the way until he had pressed a cry out of her at the reverberation of sensation he rocked through her.

He stiffened and she frantically caught at him. "Yes, Gabriel. *Yes.* Keep going."

His rhythm became elemental and primitive, yet sumptuous. It wasn't a destination, it was a place, a glorious place where they existed together. Where her entire being was filled with light. Any shadows that remained were the long, sweet shadows of summer evenings. The kind cast by a full moon when darkness reigned but pale white shapes existed.

On his skin she smelled earth and fire, metal and rain. She embraced him and pulled him deeper into the well of herself. He growled and tipped up her chin and licked at her neck, said things she didn't understand, but knew in her soul to be true.

The friction burned intimate places, the impact was nearly unbearable in its intensity, but she couldn't get enough, couldn't touch enough of him, hold him tight enough. She made her own wordless noises, primitive and feline, clenching in ecstasy while his strength held her in place for that relentless, thrilling pleasure. It was exquisite and agonizing and she wanted it to go on forever.

But she couldn't subsist in this state of tension and acute sensations. She was going to suffocate or break or her heart would explode.

And then it did. Her entire world contracted to a fine dark point, then burst. She was flame and gold and joy. Naked and pure and new.

As the most powerful release of his life receded, and Luli's sobs of culmination settled to soft, ragged breaths, an incredible sense of peace fell over him.

Gabriel somehow managed to withdraw and discard the condom, then pulled her across him, damp and sweet-smelling as the sheets beneath them. She made a contented noise and her lips touched his chest before she sighed and relaxed into a doze. He was aware of warmth and the pressure of her against him, the tickle of her hair against his naked arm, the weight of her thigh on his and an encroaching sense of regret.

His *sifu* would berate him for losing focus and letting his discipline lapse, for allowing his ego and bodily hungers to rule him. He was guilty of all those things. He'd been desperate to feast upon her. He had wanted the smug satisfaction in knowing *he* had initiated her to these pleasures and had done it *well*.

It had come at a cost. The walls he kept so impermeable around himself were weakening. The first knock had come when she had locked him out of his own software. Sections of mortar between the bricks had disintegrated under the tears she had shed against his chest that night in Paris. The winds of Africa had eroded those bricks further, as her joy at the beauty of the earth and earthly pleasures had reminded him that this world was more than greed and users and privilege.

Now she had rocked his foundation with such power he could feel the fissures extending through him.

Because she had wanted to know what it would feel like if someone loved her.

He worked his fingers into her thick hair and turned his mouth to press a kiss into the fragrant mass, wanting to shelter her even as he wanted to ravish her again.

For this privilege, he would give her almost anything.

Except his heart.

He hoped like hell it would be enough.

Luli lingered over her morning routine, feeling shy. Gabriel had woken her a few hours before dawn with kisses and caresses that had had her reaching for his turgid shape, so fascinating with velvety skin over hot iron. She had gloried in knowing how to touch him in a way he liked. They had fondled and kissed until she was burning and molten.

Then he'd slid sweetly into her and stayed there, rocking lazily.

Each time she climaxed he asked, *More?*

And she had greedily said, *Yes.*

The fourth time he had shattered with her.

She was sore, but not sorry. She felt languid and pleased and filled with mysterious knowledge.

She suspected she was in love.

It was such a new emotion, she had to pause and examine it, try to understand how its rough edges fit inside her and why it felt heavier than the ring he'd given her.

Most of all, she tried to understand how love was something she had wanted all her life and now, as she glimpsed it, it wasn't something that nestled into her and made her feel safe. It wasn't a state of being, like contentment. It was something to be given away. It was an active emotion, flowing outward, striving to reach the man who had sparked it, wherever he was at this moment.

She wanted him to love her, but strangely, even more than that, she wanted him to let her love *him*. She wanted him to welcome this overwhelming spill of feeling she wanted to pour over him.

She had tried that once, though. Her mother hadn't had a use for her heart. She'd put it on a plane to Singapore and never asked for it back.

A wrenching pain went through her as she thought of Gabriel rejecting her love. Given his childhood, she understood his reservations. It made her want to throw herself further into the fire with him. Somehow heal his pain.

But she also understood that she had to be strong. She couldn't be the girl who had become a pawn because she was afraid to be on her own. She could love him, but she couldn't be a slave to that love.

Drawing a shaky breath to bolster herself, she went down to breakfast in her robe.

"I wasn't sure if you'd still be here," she murmured, joining him at the table. It was almost ten.

"Why is Marco making you a lunch appointment with that professor from last night?" He glanced up from his tablet, took in her light makeup and the hair she'd pulled into a clip. His gaze lingered on her mouth until her lips tingled.

Then he seemed to gather himself behind

an invisible wall. He looked into her eyes, seeking an answer to his question.

"Pardon? Oh, um, he wants to talk to me about modeling opportunities. I said he should get in touch with my assistant. I didn't think he was serious. Do you mind?"

"No." He spoke abruptly, sounded like he minded. "Don't rush into anything, though. He might know people, but he might just want to be seen with you. Make sure he knows you don't need the money and you're doing him a favor by showing up."

So cynical. She bit back a sigh.

"Then I should let him buy my lunch because I don't actually *have* money?"

"You have a credit card and a generous allowance. If you want to carry cash, send Marco to the bank to withdraw some."

She shook her head as she drew her napkin onto her lap. "I crossed out the allowance on the contract and put a question mark beside it. I expected we would discuss it, but we got married and here we are."

"I wrote it back in with an extra zero. Pay attention to what you sign. This lunch is a bad idea if you won't even do that much."

"Gabriel, you know that makes me uncomfortable! I don't want *things*—" She cut herself off as she turned over her coffee cup and discovered the diamond earrings on the saucer.

All their intimacy came back in a rush. Her uninhibited clinging to him, begging for more. She had offered him her soul last night and he was giving her…crushed carbon.

Because he thought that was all he was worth? All he *had* to give?

Her mouth felt wobbly as she picked up one platinum shank. The diamond caught the sunlight and winked rainbow sparks.

"I said only if you want me to have them." The words scraped like sandpaper in the back of her throat. She had wanted to know what it felt like to be loved and instead she felt cheated.

"I do." Something in his guarded tone put a sharp vice around her heart.

This was a warning, she instinctively recognized. He would give her diamonds and limitless credit cards, but nothing more. That was the deal.

Meanwhile, she had given him her passion, her virginity, and wanted to give him so much more.

He hadn't said she couldn't, she realized.

"I'll accept them," she decided, swallowing the lump in her throat. Her voice stayed husky. "Do you know why?"

His brows went up in cautious inquiry.

"Because someday, long after our hideously civil divorce, when I'm old and gray and feeling sentimental, I'll put them on. My daughter will ask me where I got them and I'll say, *Your father would never let me wear them while he was alive. He knew it made me think of my first husband with deep fondness.*" Love. So much love. Her whole body ached with it. "But I won't tell her why that memory was such a good one, because there are some things children don't want to know about their mothers."

His expression didn't change, but his cheek ticked. "I thought you didn't want children."

She shrugged. "I'll still think of last night every time I wear these."

She put them on and deliberately met his gaze, confident that now, so would he.

You have violated our terms of service. Your access has been revoked. Join me in the tenth-floor conference room.

"What? Why? *Argh.*" She knew immediately what had happened. She had run an update this morning and Gabriel's software had overwritten all her code. She couldn't restore from backup, either. She didn't have access.

Devastated by the white screen and the stark note, she gave her useless keyboard a few more random stabs with her finger, then picked it up and rattled it in frustration.

"Mrs. Dean?" Marco appeared in her door like one of those cartoon characters that defied time and space, conjuring himself from thin air in time to say his line. "I'll call IT."

Good luck.

"No. Show me where the tenth-floor conference room is, please. And *please* call me Luli."

"Mr. Dean is the only one who calls you that. I presumed it was an endearment." He cleared his throat, then tacked on, "Ma'am."

An endearment? Gabriel had just nuked her ability to do the only job she had ever had—after picking away at it until it was down to bare bones. In the week they'd been here, he'd had her unload several investments, moving the cash into his own coffers. He'd had all the payroll records moved to his central accounting department. The property managers of Mae's various complexes now answered to someone else and even Luli's emails were cc'd to others.

"Will you go with me to my lunch tomorrow?" she asked Marco while they were in the elevator.

"Of course."

"I'm not sure how to get around the city. You could show me how the subway works."

He chuckled, then sobered with a start. "I'm sorry. I didn't realize you were serious." He shot out a hand to hold the elevator door while she stepped out. "You have full use of Mr. Dean's car. Why would you take the subway?"

Because she had to learn. She might love the man, but this marriage wouldn't last and she refused to be dependent on him.

"This is it." He paused at the first door and placed his hand on the latch and opened it.

"We'll talk about the lunch when I get back upstairs," she said over her shoulder as she entered. "Oh." She checked as she discovered at least fifty people in the room. "Hello." She took refuge in her stage persona, pasting on a smile.

They all stared at her with mouths hanging open, tracking her as she proceeded in a graceful walk down the aisle against the wall. They were seated theatre-style facing Gabriel. He stood in front of a projection screen that showed the note he'd placed on her screen to bring her here.

A public dressing down? Really?

"Why so shocked?" he asked the room.

"Beauty does not preclude brains. Thank you for coming." He took her hand as she arrived beside him. "Luli, meet my software-development team. Or rather, the lead technicians for the various modules and apps. These men and women oversee between fifty and a hundred coders each, but you're looking at my best and brightest."

His tone held an edge that made the entire room sink down in their seats.

Luli eyed him with suspicion as she made herself smile warmly and say, "Good afternoon."

"I've been showing them how you tailored our software for my grandmother, the entry points you used and some samples of the code you wrote."

He tapped his laptop and she looked over her shoulder at the string of script she had used to lock him out.

"We've been enjoying a little team-building exercise here. It took this room's collective intelligence two hours to get past your gatekeeper and lock you out."

"Your grandmother was very cautious," she prevaricated, drawing her hand from his and clasping hers lightly together before her. "I was protecting her interests, not hacking into your system."

"No, but you could. And there aren't many hackers at your level, but the fact you got this far means every one of our customers is vulnerable." His words left a resounding silence. "I wrote some rough and dirty patches while we were in Africa. That's what we pushed to the update this morning. It's going to impact functionality until it's cleaned up and tailored. I'd like you to oversee that."

She actually looked to her left to see who he was talking to because he couldn't possibly be speaking to *her*. A couple of people snickered.

"Um…" She touched the fine hairs at the back of her neck. Oversee three or four thousand people? Wasn't there an expression about trees and barking up wrong ones?

"And when people suggest I made my wife the new VP of software development because she's my wife, what will you say?" he asked the room at large.

Silence, then a lone voice said, "Actually she's a genius and made us all look like tools."

"She did, indeed. But she'll soon make you look like rock stars," he promised. "See how good she makes me look?" He held out his arm.

She went to him, pulled by forces greater

than herself to press against him, but she tilted an admonishing look up at him. Smiled brightly.

"Can I speak to you?"

CHAPTER TEN

GABRIEL BROUGHT HER into his office and closed the door.

"I realize I blindsided you with that," he acknowledged, appreciating that she had kept her cool in front of the team. That roll-with-the-punches ability of hers was one of the reasons he'd decided to give her this level of responsibility. "They needed to be humbled, though. I wanted them to accept you by your work before they knew who had outsmarted them."

"How you run your business is your business, but don't drag me into it without asking me first." She didn't balk at revealing her flustered reaction now they were alone, which was oddly endearing. He liked being privy to the woman behind the goddess she presented to the world.

"You wanted a job," he reminded her. "This is a good one."

"It's a huge one! Gabriel, you heard me this morning with the maid. I have a hard time asking someone to iron a wrinkle from my skirt. I can't supervise a *department*."

Gabriel had enjoyed eavesdropping on the power struggle as Luli attempted to pry the location of the iron from the maid while the young woman had earnestly, politely and vehemently insisted she be allowed to do her job.

"You're uniquely qualified for this position. You know the vulnerabilities and will be creative and thorough in fixing them. When you know what you want, you have no problem going after it. You even stand up to me to get it. You'll be fine."

"Yes, well, that's the issue. I don't want it."

"You don't want this exceptionally good job I'm giving you."

"Giving," she repeated. "So this *is* nepotism."

"No." He took a firmer grip on his patience. "I just explained why I chose you."

"Do *I* get a choice? Is it an offer or an order?"

"It's an offer with a salary of a quarter million dollars attached to it." Why was she fighting him? Did she not realize they would work together every day?

"Oh, that does stink of nepotism."

"Call a headhunter." He pointed at the telephone. "It's competitive, not outrageous."

"You call a headhunter," she muttered. "I can make twice that staying home with my feet up, waiting for my allowance to roll in."

He threw up his hands, truly baffled by this woman.

"In Singapore, you said you were proving your skills to me," he reminded her. "You have. You just proved them to a roomful of top-notch programmers. I'm offering you a job in this field and you're refusing it?"

"For how long, Gabriel?"

The barb of sadness in her voice caught in his heart, pulling him up short.

"Will I be able to finish before our marriage is over? Will you still want me here when we're divorced? Will you trust me not to move on to some competitor with what I know? You don't want me that deeply entwined in your livelihood. I know you don't. That's why you've spent every day since we met prying me out of it."

He squeezed the back of his neck. Had he thought that far ahead? Only insofar as to think that maybe, if enough incentives were offered, she would stay here. In his office, in his home, in his bed.

"We could have a successful marriage, Luli."

"Provided I give you babies and never expect anything more of you than having my physical needs met. I have other needs, Gabriel." Her soft voice and the quiet torment in her gaze were too much to face.

He turned to the window.

After a moment, her footsteps padded toward him. Her arms came around his waist and the weight of her head settled between his shoulder blades.

"I'm always going to wonder who I'm supposed to be. Not the person my mother or Mae or you turned me into. The person I make of myself. I have to do that."

"By turning yourself into an object in front of cameras?"

"Maybe. At least it would be my choice."

He looked at her hands folded across his middle, his ring bright on her finger. He could give her his heart or her freedom.

He swallowed, picked up her hands and brought them to his mouth, kissing the inside of each wrist.

"Do what you need to do, then," he said, even though the words burned like acid through his torso. "I'll find someone else."

"Thank you. Oh, shoot." She drew back

and brushed her fingers in the middle of his spine. "I got lipstick on your shirt. You'll have to change it. Sorry."

He turned and looped his arms around her lower back, pulling her in again to ease the line of pain still burning down his center. "You know what people are going to think if I change my shirt after a private meeting with my wife in my office."

"That I threw my coffee at you?" Her lips tilted into the seductive smile that tightened his skin all over his body.

She twined her arms around his neck, crushing her breasts to his chest, growing more self-assured in her feminine power by the day. He thrilled at this brazen side of her. It allowed him to unleash his appetites to the fullest, confident she would slow him down if he became too aggressive.

He slid his hands under her ass and lifted, swelling with invincible strength. Her skirt rode up and she wrapped her thighs in a squeeze around his waist.

He could have taken her to his sofa, but he took her to his desk. It wasn't as comfortable, but as he pressed her onto her back against his blotter, and her earrings winked at him, he knew he would think of her every single time he sat here.

It was foolish and sentimental and self-destructive to want her memory to infuse his private space, but he did. He wanted her everywhere. Her scent on his body, her long hairs on his sleeve, her teeth marks in his shoulder and her hot breath against his ear.

He needed all these things because one day it would be all he had.

That realization slowed him down.

Much as he wanted to strip her naked and drive into her and *make* her his, he was suddenly gripped by a deeper need. One that demanded he take his time, immerse himself in every caress, wring the furthest reaches of pleasure from her with each kiss and tantalizing touch.

He smoothed his lips across her nipples through her shirt, making her writhe, and made her turn her head so he could unpin her hair, then ran his fingers through the mass that made him crazy, every single time he came near her.

He kissed her tenderly and smiled with satisfaction when she tried to urge him along, driving her tongue into his mouth and reaching for his belt.

He wanted to tell her how beautiful she was, how much pleasure he wanted to give her. Words tangled into a fiery knot in his throat while flames continued to lick inside his chest, branding her deep behind his breastbone where she would stay imprinted forever.

He hurt. Deep inside, he ached with emptiness. The only way to assuage that ache was this. Touch her, bare her, hold her. Cover her and press into her and stay there, unmoving while he kissed her long and slow, drugging both of them with this potent magic they created.

And when she quivered on the knife's edge with him, when the borders of reality smudged and time ceased to exist, he gathered her up so they were eye to eye as the fire consumed them in a golden shimmer that, he knew, would bind him to her forever.

Three weeks later, with great excitement, Luli sat for a test shoot. Not wanting to spend Gabriel's money, she gave students from the professor's school an opportunity to build their own portfolio while starting hers. A handful of designers, stylists and photographers had given her a taste of the grueling work that was the inside view of modeling.

The end result was a selection of photos from classic perfume ad fare to an avant-garde shot of her in smeared makeup with a roller still stuck in her hair and a tinfoil robe hanging off one shoulder.

Gabriel didn't say much beyond, "The clamor to represent you won't have anything to do with me. You're very photogenic."

She hadn't expected him to gush, but she had hoped for more. A deep chasm had begun opening since the day they had made love in his office. He swore he wasn't angry that she hadn't taken the job he'd offered. He agreed that he would prefer to keep his business separate from her, now that Mae's holdings had been absorbed into his own.

Luli kept trying to bring them closer with lovemaking and it worked temporarily, but always made the separation afterward more painful than if they'd maintained their individuality in the first place.

It was becoming clear to her that his prediction was true. She wanted his love and he couldn't offer it. It was agony to be denied his heart and for that reason, she had to begin building the life she would have when their marriage was over. At least a demanding schedule of working away would give her some distance from the pain and provide an excuse for the inevitable publicity when the time came.

"I've decided to take the job in Milan," she

told him as they dressed to go to a Broadway premiere.

She saw his hand check as he reached for a shirt on a hanger. He wore only a towel. His lean back was a study in animal beauty, flaring upward from his hips to wide shoulders and muscles that twisted as he pulled the shirt free.

"I'll leave Saturday morning so I'm well rested and ready to work on Monday."

Please tell me not to go, she silently pleaded. *Tell me you can't live without me.*

"You're not flying commercial."

"First class. They're paying for Marco to go with me." Among Marco's many talents, she had learned he also ensured her physical safety. Gabriel had never been a target for kidnapping or other threats, but given his position, he took precautions. She and Marco were becoming friends so she didn't mind that he was her constant companion when Gabriel wasn't with her.

"Take the jet."

At a million dollars per nautical mile?

"They've already made the arrangements. There's no reason you should be out of pocket."

"I don't care about the money."

"What *do* you care about?" she blurted, and regretted it immediately.

Especially when he dragged in a breath that hissed.

"What do you want me to say, Luli? You've put me in a no-win situation. If I ask you not to work, I'm holding you back. If I let you go, I'm abandoning you."

"It *is* a win for you, though," she insisted with a spark of temper. "You didn't want me in the first place. I'm leaving, giving you the solitude you prefer and you're not even *thanking* me." Her voice started to break.

She walked out of the closet and strode down the hall to her room. She might sleep in his bed, but all her clothes were in here. Not even her dental floss had made it into his treasured private space.

"I told you," he said, following her to brace his arms in the open doorway of her room. "I told you this was how it would be."

"Yes, you tried to be *so* honorable and save me from my silly romantic notions that you might actually come to care for me." She took a shaky breath and flipped her hair back behind her shoulder. "You're right, okay? It is painful to have feelings for someone. No matter how loved you make me feel when we're in bed, the pain comes back afterward when I remember you don't. That's why I'm leaving. And I'll take every job they will throw

at me to keep from coming back here and…
wishing."

"Luli—" He hung his head.

"Don't worry about it, Gabriel. You can't
make someone love you. I accepted that a
long time ago. But I do have to stop trying."
She swallowed. "I'd rather not go out if you
don't mind. I'm going to have a bath and an
early night." She locked herself into the bathroom.

He stirred, aching with arousal, and reached
for her.

She wasn't here.

Gabriel snapped awake and groaned like an
injured animal, wondering how he was going
to cope with even one more day of this. It had
been six and he was dying.

Withering.

It wasn't just sexual hunger, although he
missed the physical release. Everything about
the act. Everything about her. He missed
her—the feel of her skin against his own,
her weight on the mattress beside him, her
smile across the table and her laughter echoing from far down a hall.

*You can't make someone love you. But I do
have to stop trying.*

The anguish that had gripped him as she

said that had been nearly unbearable. He didn't want her to stop trying. Did she think he didn't notice when she stroked her fingers across his shoulders, simply because she was passing behind where he was seated? Or that she wore those damned earrings at the most ridiculous times, most certainly to get the best possible rise out of him? She flirted and cuddled and kept him on his toes.

It was painful to have feelings for someone. He had always known that love hurt. But was he making both of them suffer just to prove he was right?

He sure as hell hadn't spared himself any pain by holding her off. She had acted like she was doing him a favor by leaving and he had tried to convince himself he didn't want her to stay.

But he did. He needed her. Like air and water and sunlight.

Throwing off his covers, he picked up his phone, trying to think what he'd say to her if she answered. It was midmorning in Milan. She was probably already working.

He tapped to wake the screen and read a text from Marco that stopped his heart.

CHAPTER ELEVEN

IT HAD ALREADY been an impossibly long day, but Luli dug deep and conjured a sultry expression, lips parted with invitation only a hair's breadth from her fellow model's. He was a gorgeous Italian whose smoky stare drifted toward Marco every time they took a break, but he made his passion for her seem real as he clutched her close and bent dominantly over her.

"What the *hell*?"

Gabriel's voice jolted through the studio, halting the rapid click of the camera shutter. Her partner tightened his hold on her, helping her straighten and catch her balance. Then he angled her away from Gabriel as he strode toward them looking like he would take them both apart.

"Sir!" Marco raced forward to intercept him.

"Gabriel!" Luli extricated herself from the Italian's hold. "What are you doing here?"

"What are *you* doing?"

"Working. Obviously."

He gave the Italian a filthy look that suggested he didn't care for her type of "work," but only asked, "Why?"

"What do you mean, why?"

"Sir—" The photographer was taking a tone. Even worse, he was glaring at Luli as though he blamed her for the interruption.

"I'm sorry—I texted him," Marco said, holding up his hands. "This is my fault. I was worried," he added in a gentle apology directed at Luli. Then he smiled placatingly at Gabriel. "They're almost finished. We can wait outside."

"I'll wait right here." He crossed his arms and stood with his toes mere inches from the carpet of the set.

Luli shouldn't have been surprised Marco had told Gabriel that her mother had died. For years, she had set alerts to pick up her mother's name, but yesterday's had been the first in ages to ping a headline about her. Her death after a medical complication had been noted by the Venezuelan press because she had once been a renowned beauty, but details had been scant.

Luli had mentioned it to Marco, though, and asked him to prepare a statement in the unlikely case the connection was discovered by an overzealous reporter. He had pointed out her contract allowed for family emergency and bereavement leave, but she was too early in this new career of hers to be anything but unrelentingly reliable.

Besides, the news changed nothing.

She should have realized Marco would warn Gabriel of the potential media storm. Had something leaked into the press? Was that why he was stomping in here, breathing fire?

She couldn't think about that right now. She had to do what she was paid to do.

Thirty minutes later they wrapped. As she changed, she heard Gabriel ask Marco, "What the hell are they even selling with all that sex?"

Marco cleared his throat. "The handbag on the chair."

The resounding silence that followed that statement told her what Gabriel thought of *that*.

Marco apologized to her again when she rejoined them.

"It's fine. We both know who pays your salary." She freed her hair from the collar of her light coat.

"Mrs. Dean." He put out a hand in a plea.

"You were upset. I could see it even if the camera couldn't."

And he thought she and Gabriel had a relationship that included endearments and a deeper caring than it did.

"I'm fine," she assured Marco with a faint smile. "Take the evening off. Enjoy the city." Enjoy the Italian.

She went back to her hotel with Gabriel, the silence between them thick as gelatin.

As the door closed behind him, Gabriel was the first to speak, asking tightly, "Why are you angry Marco told me?"

"Why are *you* angry?" The hollow sensation in the base of her throat was spreading into her chest cavity, growing too big to suppress or ignore.

"Because you didn't tell me yourself. Why didn't you?"

Something broke inside her, sending a flood of anguished emotion through her. Not at the knowledge her mother was dead, but at the other knowledge that had struck like a blow when she had considered telling Gabriel.

"I didn't think you'd care."

He closed his eyes in a way that suggested she had run him through.

"I'm not trying to make you feel guilty,"

she muttered, biting her lip. "I'm not trying to make you feel anything."

"And yet I feel like hell," he bit out. "She doesn't deserve your grief, Luli."

"I know that." She realized she was convulsively opening and shutting the clasp on her purse. She threw it into a chair.

"And yet you still grieve."

"That's why you're angry? I can't help how I feel, Gabriel!"

"Neither can I! That's why I'm angry. At myself. I knew immediately that you'd be hurting and I wasn't here for you."

"*You* hurt me," she reminded wildly, instantly plunged back into the despair of their last conversation.

"I know that," he thundered. "I stood there and saw that I was turning a knife in you exactly as you are turning one in me right now. I hate that we can do this to each other."

Her eyes grew wet. She turned away, thinking that she had known this was coming, but she couldn't bear it. "Please don't say it," she begged, agonized.

"Say what? That I love you? I do. I *love* you, Luli."

Her heart swerved. "What?"

She came around cautiously, dizzy, certain

she had misheard. "I thought you were going to say it's over."

"Like hell. This will never be over." He dragged in a tormented breath, face contorting with pained acceptance. "I have never wanted to say those words to anyone. I knew it would be pure torture to feel it."

She inhaled at that gut punch.

He closed the distance in a few strides and picked up her hands, holding on to them when she tried to pull away.

"Love forces you to feel that other person's heartbeat. When they cry, you cry. When you hurt them, that pain comes back on you tenfold." He drew her closer, so he cupped her hand against his heart and cradled the side of her face with his other palm.

"But when they're happy, you're so happy you can't contain it. When they give you their heart, there isn't enough room in your own body for both. You have to give up yours or the imbalance will break both of you."

"You have my heart."

"I know. It's better than the one I had." His thumb grazed her cheek in a tender caress. "Lighter, softer. God knows it's prettier. Take mine. Fix it. Make it shine."

She had to bite her lips to steady them. Her eyes were so wet, she could hardly see the light gleaming in his gaze, but she felt it beaming through her, filling her until she glowed. "It's just rusty," she choked. "But it works."

"You make me happy, Luli. Too happy. If I ever lose you, I'll become the emotional cripple my father became. That terrifies me." His expression spasmed with deep emotion. "But pushing you away is killing me. I cannot bear the pain of hurting you."

It didn't escape her that he was giving her the one thing he had never wanted to give up. She was awed by the gift of his love and could only return it with the embrace of her arms, the press of her lips to his, the promise of forever that pulsed in her heart.

"Say it," he whispered against her cheek.

"I love you, Gabriel. I love you with every breath in my body. I always will."

"I love you, too. Infinitely."

Their words seemed to infuse the air around them, gaining strength from the whispers and friction of their two bodies embracing. From the meeting of their soft gazes across the narrow space, and the unspoken desire that had them moving to the bedroom in perfect accord to celebrate their union in the most ancient and exalted of forms.

EPILOGUE

"Shh..." Gilly said, holding her stubby little finger against her pursed lips.

"That's right. We're quiet when we feed the fish," Gabriel said in the warm, patient tone he always used with their daughter.

"Gen-tow," Gilly said, and carefully pinched the food from his palm and released it into the tank he had placed in her room days after she was born.

Luli hung back at the door, heart so full when she watched them, she nearly cried over it, every single day. Gabriel teased her if he caught her, but if he happened to walk in on tai chi practice, when their toddler tried to follow her mother's moves with her still clumsy, yet determined little limbs, he was as likely to grow misty as he was to step in and join them.

They were both utterly enamored with their little girl, in a state of perpetual wonderment that they had made something so exquisitely perfect from the earthy, greedy hunger that never let up between them.

"Mama!" Gilly noticed her and beamed her teensy white teeth.

"Hi, baby." Luli moved to catch the sprite as she threw herself from her father's arms and squeezed Luli's neck with exuberance.

Gabriel dropped a smiling kiss against her lips.

"She's been asking for you. I was about to send a search party."

"Blame your coders."

"Anything I should know about?"

"No, I can handle it." She had kept up the modeling for a year, sticking with local shoots unless Gabriel had been able to travel with her. When her pregnancy started showing, she quit and stayed home for almost a year, taking a lead role in some of Gabriel's charities before beginning work on an app to make donations easier to request, track and disperse.

Gabriel had talked her into developing it with his team and she'd been working with them ever since.

"Pwetty," Gilly said, drawing back to touch one of Luli's earrings.

"Let's wash your hands," Gabriel said, catching her fishy fingers. "Those are special."

"Why?" Gilly was at the age when she liked to ask that question *a lot.*

"Would you like to field this one?" Gabriel invited Luli with a knowing smirk as he took their daughter from her.

"Daddy gave them to me the night I fell in love with him," she told Gilly.

"Is that what happened that night?" Gabriel teased. "I remembered something else, but okay."

"That you fell in love with me, too?" she guessed with a sly smile.

"That was it." He dropped another kiss on her lips. "That is exactly what happened that night."

* * * * *

If you enjoyed
Untouched Until Her Ultra-Rich Husband
you're sure to enjoy these other stories
by Dani Collins!

Sheikh's Princess of Convenience
Claiming His Christmas Wife
A Virgin to Redeem the Billionaire
Innocent's Nine-Month Scandal

Available now!